"Please don't deceive yourself, my love...."

Gabriel lowered his dark head, his warm breath fanning Fay's cheek as he spoke. "Admit it, Fay," he said thickly. "You want me."

Fay felt the violent passion in him as their lips met. Her love was too strong to deny him, and she whispered his name over and over.

"Tell me now," he groaned. "Tell me now that you don't want me."

Fay stared at him with wide bitter eyes. Yes, she wanted him—she was desperate for him, but she would never admit it. Gathering all her strength she turned and fled, not looking back until she'd reached the front door. He had not moved. He stood on the hill watching her, his body tall and still with a nameless defeat.

She had lied again....

PATRICIA LAKE

perfect passion

Harlequin Books

TORONTO • LONDON • LOS ANGELES • AMSTERDAM
SYDNEY • HAMBURG • PARIS • STOCKHOLM • ATHENS • TOKYO

Harlequin Presents edition published May 1982
ISBN 0-373-10501-0

Original hardcover edition published in 1981
by Mills & Boon Limited

CHAPTER ONE

As she glanced up idly, Fay's eyes once again encountered those of a pleasant-looking fair young man seated opposite to her in the compartment. She smiled coolly, leaving him in no doubt that any conversation was out of the question, and averted her gaze to the window. The rugged countryside speeding by was truly beautiful, she thought absently, as she settled into a more comfortable position on her seat. It was almost a luxury to travel by train, after the dirt and madness of driving in London traffic.

Her eyes closed wearily, the speed of the train having a soporific effect on her, and she pulled the soft fur collar of her coat up around her neck. She felt tired and rather weak—there was little doubt that she needed a rest, away from the city, and everything. Although fully recovered from the bout of pneumonia that had laid her up for months, she was still easily exhausted, often tired and lethargic, and had jumped at the chance of a convalescence period at her aunt's lovely country home.

The train pulled into a small and deserted country station, and Fay glanced at the name. The next stop would be hers. Good. She was so looking forward to seeing Sophie again.

The young man opposite got to his feet, pulling down a small leather suitcase from the luggage rack above his head. He smiled sweetly and regretfully at Fay as he made his way to the door, and she smiled back brightly, thankful that he had not been persistent. He reminded her a little of Sam—her thoughts turned to him almost reluctantly, as the train began to move again.

Despite their bitter, hurtful row, Sam had wanted to drive her up here to Yorkshire, but she had refused, feeling very guilty at the obvious disappointment on his face, trying to make him understand that a clean break was for the best, just then. Perhaps this short time away from her usual day-to-day environment would help her sort out her rather confused feelings for Sam.

The Daileys had lived next door to the Drummonds since before Fay had been born, and because the families were close friends, it was natural that Fay and Sam, growing up together, should become close, their deep friendship developing into something stronger as time passed.

Sam had made it clear that he wanted to marry her, and indeed, both families expected it, but something deep inside Fay had held back. Was it what she wanted? she asked herself now. Sighing, she knew that it was not. She loved Sam, of course, but instinct told her that it was love for a brother. They had become unofficially engaged, partly, as Fay now realised, because she could not bear to hurt him—a cowardly, selfish reason for taking the easy way out. And maybe it had been nerves, or a lingering depression from her illness, but she had suddenly seen the whole situation in perspective. She had instinctively recoiled from the idea of publicly announcing their engagement, and had known at that moment that she could never marry Sam. As she tried to explain this to him, he had refused to take her seriously at first, teasing her in his gentle way about her fear of being tied down—reassuring her. In the end, though, she had forced him to see that she was serious and would not marry him. She had been rather unkind, she knew now, and a fierce and angry row had ensued. This was the reason that she had decided to take up her aunt's offer of a long holiday in Yorkshire.

Sam had turned up at her flat the following evening, to find her packing, and although he had seemed pale and resigned she had known, when he offered her a lift, that he was hoping to win her round. She knew him too well, and this had prompted her refusal. Miserably, she wondered why honesty demanded such a high price, remembering Sam's hurt eyes as he had slammed from her flat. She seemed incapable of being honest or of loving to her full capacity, always holding back from becoming too involved. Even with Sam she had been perhaps a little dishonest. She did trust him, though, probably because she had known him all her life, and he knew all about her, all her fears. He had been an easy way out, and with new insight she realised that was why she had let him believe, let herself believe, that she would marry him. Fortunately, she had even held back on this marriage, her love and respect for Sam had overcome her fear, and had stopped her using him just in time.

Fay had a deep-rooted mistrust of all men, stemming from an awful, fateful night when she was twelve years old. She would never forget sitting on the stairs, having been woken by the noise from below, silent tears trickling down her face, as she listened with disbelieving horror to her mother crying and shouting hysterically, and her father coldly and angrily admitting his affair with another woman.

Fay's safe secure world had fallen about her ears, and not knowing or understanding the full story, she had seen only her unnaturally quiet, brokenhearted mother in the months that followed. Life and laughter had gone, her mother was a different person, and Fay, confused and terribly upset, had vowed never to forgive her father. She had been shocked by his cruelty, his deceit, and the whole episode had left her emotionally scarred and deeply distrusting.

Although her parents had split up for a short time, her mother had taken her father back, much to Fay's amazement, and things had returned almost to normal outwardly, though the once happy, carefree atmosphere in the house was lost for ever, and her mother became colder and more detached, somehow different.

Fay had tried, but could not change her attitude towards men. She automatically froze advances, fiercely attacking any man who tried to break down her carefully constructed barriers. What had happened to her mother would never happen to her. Her heart was whole and untouched and that was the way she intended to keep it.

Still pondering on her own weakness, she noticed that the train was slowing down. This was her station, and jumping to her feet she pulled down her two suitcases, with some difficulty, and struggled on to the platform with them. Would Sophie be here to meet her? One thing was certain, she could not carry these suitcases very far.

She shivered uncontrollably as the train began moving away. The platform was almost deserted, and light snow was beginning to fall, eerie in the tiring grey light of a winter afternoon.

Fay pulled her thick coat tighter around herself, and pulled on her bright, warm Fair Isle gloves. There was no sign of her aunt, and ridiculously, tears began welling up in her eyes. She knew from experience that there was no taxi or bus service from this tiny country station and Sophie did not have a telephone, which was madness in this day and age, she thought irritably, brushing away her tears with angry fingers. What would she do? There was no way she could walk to

Lambrigg House, certainly not carrying her cases. She took a deep breath—she really would have to pull herself together. Her imagination was running riot, as she imagined herself stranded. Sophie will be here any minute, she told herself sternly. The snow will have held her up.

She knew the roads were bad at this time of year. Panicking irrationally at the thought of her aunt crashing the car, she looked around, hoping for some sign of her. There was none, but her eyes fell on the tall figure of a man, indistinct in the dim afternoon light, leaning indolently against a wall behind her. Watching her. Even as she looked at him, he began to stroll towards her and for a split second she was held spellbound, fascinated by the lithe grace of his movement, before turning quickly away. This was the last thing she wanted, to be pestered by an unknown man on this dark deserted station—even if he did move beautifully. Her eyes scanned the platform, looking in vain for a porter, a ticket-collecter—any station official, as almost fearfully she sensed the man just behind her. And although she told herself wryly that it was just her overwrought and tired imagination again she was ready for flight, as he finally spoke.

'Miss Drummond?' His voice was low, attractive and slightly mocking. He saw the fear on her face as she spun round, her emerald eyes huge and questioning in her pale, vulnerable face. He was looking down at her watchfully, his dark face closed and unfathomable, waiting for her answer, and all she could do was to gaze up at him speechlessly. Even in the dim light, his face held her still, deep inside. Although she could not see him clearly, the hard, lean bones of his face, shadowed and inexplicably mysterious, suddenly made Fay's heart beat faster. She lowered her head, with some effort, blushing furiously in the knowledge that she had been staring at him, and took a deep breath.

'Who are you?' she whispered huskily, the words sticking in her throat, still unable to meet his eyes.

'Does it matter? I'm afraid your aunt couldn't meet you, so I've come instead,' he answered cryptically, his voice distant and faintly bored, easily giving the impression that he considered her to be wasting his time. He picked up her suitcases effortlessly.

'The car is over here,' he said curtly, and without waiting for her began to walk away. Fay stood still for a moment trying to gather her scattered thoughts, her eyes still watching the tall dark man disappearing out of the station with her suitcases. Who on earth was he? she wondered as she began to follow him out of the station to a Land Rover, obviously his, parked near the entrance.

His manners certainly left a lot to be desired, she thought grimly, as without speaking, he motioned her into the car, after placing her cases in the back. She got in, staring straight ahead, feeling rather angry and not a little piqued as she heard the man sliding into the seat beside her, switching on the engine.

Without moving her head, she glanced at him surreptitiously from beneath her eyelashes. His profile was strong and proud, and loath as she was to admit it, extremely attractive, stirring a faint shiver of excitement inside her. She wanted to see him in the light, because in the rapidly falling darkness he seemed hard and almost menacing, and without warning, she was suddenly frightened.

Why had Sophie been unable to meet her at the station? What if this man had nothing to do with her aunt?

'Why couldn't Sophie come to meet me, and who are you?' she blurted out, unable to hold the questions inside her any longer. She turned her head towards him, her embarrassment forgotten, replaced by fear.

The man took his eyes off the road for a second and glanced at her.

'Are you afraid of me?' he asked softly, his voice threaded with amusement.

Fay's heart began beating painfully fast at something in his voice, something that she could not recognise, but something that she knew, instinctively. This was some strange game he was playing, and she wanted no part of it. She took another deep breath.

'No,' she replied steadily, 'I'm not afraid of you. I would just like to know who you are. . . .' She broke off, biting her lip savagely. Her voice was trembling and she was determined that he would not see her fear.

The Land Rover slowed suddenly, as he pulled up at the side of the road, and turned off the engine. Fay shrank into her seat as he reached up and switched on the small overhead light, turning towards her as he did so, noting her fearful movement with an amused twist of his mouth. He looked at her for a long moment before speaking, and she stared back, mesmerised by the dark glitter of his eyes.

'What's the matter with you?' he asked almost roughly. 'Why are you afraid?'

'I've told you——' she flashed, angry with him for frightening her, for being so damned attractive, 'I'm not afraid. . . .'

'Liar.' He cut across her softly, reaching across to catch her small chin gently, with long strong fingers. At his touch, shimmering fire danced on her skin, and Fay trembled, unable to push from her confused mind the image of those lean hands on her body. She shook her head wordlessly, shocked at these disturbing and intrusive thoughts, and his hand dropped from her face.

'You tremble when I touch you,' he mused gently, wonderingly.

'I'm cold, that's all,' Fay replied stiffly. 'And I think your manners are appalling Mr . . . Mr . . . Oh!' The man smiled, his eyes suddenly filled with light, and to Fay's wonder, warmth. She held her breath as they stared at each other in the dimly lit, somehow intimate car, knowing that something powerful—a strange attraction—was crackling between them, around them, binding them together.

'I'm sorry. I have been rude, and I had no intention of frightening you. You know that I won't hurt you, don't you?' he murmured, his darkly narrowed eyes sliding to her mouth, his amusement gone. Fay's heart began to race.

'Yes,' she answered immediately, positively, for she knew now that it was the truth.

He smiled them. 'I'm glad we've got that sorted out,' he said wryly. 'And my name is Winter—Gabriel Winter. Sophie will be wondering where you are. The roads are far too dangerous for her to drive,' he added, by way of an explanation for his presence.

He switched on the engine again and pulled on to the road. Their strange, exhilarating conversation seemed to be at an end, and Fay settled back into her seat relieved and at the same time disappointed. The snow was falling heavily now, and the man Gabriel Winter had all his attention focused on the road ahead. Peering through the window, Fay could see nothing but the whirling snowflakes, she could not see the road at all, and wondered how on earth they would get to Lambrigg House.

'Would you pass me a cigarette? Under there.' He indicated the dashboard and Fay reached for them.

She felt safe with him now, safe and warm in the dark cocoon of the car. She passed him a cigarette, with a smile.

'Can I have one?' she asked, wondering if she should, so soon after her illness, but suddenly needing one.

'Of course. I should have offered,' he replied politely, absently, frowning as he carefully manoeuvred the car slowly along the dark, dangerous roads. Fay struck a match and held it to his cigarette, noticing in the flare of light the hard angles of his face thrown into sharp relief, and the startling fact that his eyes were grey. She lit her own cigarette and drew on it deeply. She did not speak, aware that he needed all his concentration for his driving, but her mind was filled with him. Gabriel Winter—a man with eyes as grey as his name. His name seemed vaguely familiar, and he had said it as if he expected her to recognise it, but she could not pin it down. He was obviously a friend of Sophie's, although she could not recall any mention of him in her aunt's letters. Oh well, she would find out soon enough.

The cigarette was beginning to make her cough and she stubbed it out quickly, all at once incredibly weary. She closed her eyes for a moment, the whirling, dancing snow suddenly making her feel quite dizzy. . . .

She awoke with a start to find Gabriel Winter leaning over her, shaking her gently. For a moment she stared blankly up at him, at his dark unknown face. Then, realising that her head was cushioned against his hard shoulder, and feeling the intimate warmth of his breath fanning her cheek, she pulled herself way from him, embarrassment colouring her face.

'We're here,' he said sardonically, sliding gracefully out of the Land Rover even as he spoke.

Fay shook her head, collecting her confused and scattered thoughts, then pushed open the door, shivering at the blast of freezing cold air that hit her as she stepped outside.

Sophie was standing in the open doorway of the house, warm, bright and welcoming light spilling out around her, and Fay ran to her, aware that her every movement was being carefully watched by cool, mocking grey eyes.

'Sophie, it's so lovely to see you again!' she cried, kissing her aunt joyfully.

Sophie hugged her niece affectionately, her mild blue eyes misting.

'Fay, my dear, you're freezing! Do come inside and get warm. And you're so thin!' she exclaimed. Fay smiled at her aunt's concern, and allowed herself to be pulled into the warm bright hall.

'You must have a drink,' Sophie said firmly, then turned to shout over her shoulder to the man still waiting outside. 'Gabe—could you bring Fay's cases inside, please?' Fay heard his agreement, feeling astonished. Gabe—her aunt called him Gabe! It seemed vaguely disrespectful—she would have to get to the bottom of this.

She followed Sophie's small, bustling figure through the mellow, oak-panelled hall into a bright room with a roaring log fire. Drawn by its brightness, she walked towards it, and held out her hands for warmth. She gazed round the much-loved and well-remembered room eagerly. Nothing had changed. Her eyes scanned the tall windows with brightly-painted wooden shutters and window seats, bordered with heavy velvet curtains. The pale walls, scattered with framed photographs—Sophie's hobby—and thick Oriental carpet. Dark furniture complementing the huge carved fireplace, and chintz-covered chairs. It was a beautiful room.

'Take your coat off, Fay. Now, would you like tea, coffee, or something stronger?'

'Tea would be lovely, Sophie—just what I need after

that train journey,' Fay replied, shrugging off her heavy fur coat.

She smoothed down the richly embroidered black silk tunic, that she had teamed with black velvet trousers, under long boots, for the journey and flicked back her tousled auburn hair. She could not help feeling that she looked dreadful, although why that should worry her, at that moment, she did not like to think.

'Can I help you with the tea?' she asked, still warming her frozen hands. Sophie shook her head.

'No, it's already made—it only needs pouring. Sit down, child, you look exhausted.'

Fay sank gratefully into the soft chintz-covered armchair nearest to the fire.

'How are you, Sophie?' she asked her aunt, watching her affectionately as she busied herself with the tea tray.

'I'm fine, my dear, never better. Which is more than I can say for you, from the look of you.'

'I'm fully recovered,' Fay protested. 'I'm just easily tired—but that will pass.'

'You're skin and bone!' Sophie teased sternly, handing her a steaming cup of tea. 'I'm sorry I couldn't meet you from the station, but I daren't drive in this weather—so dangerous, and Gabe offered, so I took him up on it. You didn't mind, did you, love?'

'Of course not,' Fay lied reassuringly. 'By the way, Sophie, who is . . .?'

Her question was cut short, by the appearance of the man himself strolling gracefully into the room, filling it with his presence. Fay bowed her head immediately, and concentrated on drinking her tea.

'I've left Miss Drummond's cases in the hall. I'll take them up later,' he drawled lazily, and Fay could feel his penetrating gaze upon her as surely as if he had touched her.

'You'll have a drink?' Fay heard her aunt say.

'Scotch, please,' came the low reply.

'Are the roads very bad? It took you a long time to get here,' Sophie said, handing him a glass with a warm smile.

'Almost blocked with this latest fall. I wouldn't be surprised if we're snowed in by next week.' The laziness was gone from his voice and Fay glanced up quickly. If they were snowed in, at least she would not see him. He was far too disturbing for her peace of mind, and the less she saw of him the better.

He was deep in conversation with her aunt, and Fay took her opportunity and began a thorough, albeit discreet, inspection of this man who intrigued her so. He was very tall—well over six feet, and without his coat she could see that he was powerfully built, very strong and lean. The tall power of him made his unaffected grace, even more apparent in his casual stance, all the more remarkable. He moved like a sleek animal of prey, with economy and silence, and it took Fay's breath away.

The dark checked cotton shirt that he was wearing clung to his broad shoulders and chest, revealing the strong brown colour of his throat, and the beginnings of the short dark hairs that no doubt matted his chest. His hips were slim, his stomach flat and his legs strong, the heavy muscles of his thighs, pressing tautly against the dark material of his trousers.

Fay's inquisitive glance slid to his face—even more fascinating in the brightly-lit room. His hair was dark and thick. It touched his collar and framed his lean, proud face. Thick black eyebrows shadowed the heavy lids of his bleak grey eyes—truly remarkable eyes, thought Fay, as clear and as grey as a winter twilight. Strong, prominent almost fleshless cheekbones and a strong jaw accentuated all the hollows and angles of

his face, and his mouth was thin, hard and sensual—
perhaps a little cruel. He was not conventionally handsome, but once seen his extremely attractive face would
not easily be forgotten and he drew Fay like a magnet.
Even across the room, she could feel his powerful and
aggressive sexual aura. She would have to keep out of
his way while she was here, and she prayed that Sophie
would not invite him to stay for dinner.

She was still staring at him, discretion forgotten,
wondering at his age, having estimated it at around
thirty-five, when he turned his head towards her
slowly, sensing her gaze. Their eyes met, his narrowed
and unreadable, hers shocked and almost fearful, at
the impact he made on her. His cruel mouth twisted
mockingly, leaving her in no doubt that he had been
aware of her thorough examination of him, and Fay's
eyes dropped immediately, delicate colour staining her
pale cheeks as she cursed herself for being so obvious.
He made her feel so gauche, so naïve—she had not
blushed for years, and here she was, a twenty-five-year-
old woman acting like a fourteen-year-old schoolgirl.

Angry with herself and with him, she put down her
tea cup and got to her feet, feeling incredibly tired.
She would have a shower before dinner, by which time
Gabriel Winter should have gone. She excused herself
politely, ignoring the searching grey eyes on her face,
and asked Sophie where her room was. It was the room
she usually had when she stayed here, so she escaped
quickly, knowing where it was.

She made her way upstairs to her room and shut the
door, finding herself trembling. Damn him for un-
settling her like this!

Her room had cream walls, warm and restful. Pale
rugs contrasted vividly with dark, heavy antique furniture and the bed was big, soft and inviting with an
exquisitely carved headboard and footboard. Soft light

from two large glass lamps flooded the room peacefully, and the whole effect was quietly beautiful, balm
to her ragged nerves. Her aunt certainly had taste, Fay
thought as she wandered over to the mullioned window
and peered through. The snow was still falling, as
heavy as ever, and she pulled the heavy lace curtains
together quickly, glad to be warm and inside on such
an afternoon.

There was a small fire blazing in the tiled hearth,
and intending to take her shower, she stripped off her
clothes in front of it, basking in the warmth on her
slender body, and slipped into a pale green velvet wrap
laid out on the bed for her. Sitting on the bed, she
suddenly realised that her suitcases were still downstairs. If she went down for them now, she was bound
to be seen, and she would have to make two journeys
anyway. She would wait until Gabriel Winter left—
she could not face him—and then go down for them.
She did not intend to see him again if at all possible.
She would lie down for a moment, then go downstairs
when the coast was clear. She felt so very tired. . . .

She was woken by a sharp noise near the bed. Without opening her eyes, she arched her back, pushing
her hands through her hair. This was the second time
she had fallen asleep today; what was the matter with
her? She opened her eyes slowly, stretching languor-
ously, to find Gabriel Winter standing over her,
watching her silently, dissecting her with those clear,
hooded grey eyes. Fay froze for a second, then as anger
and embarrassment cut through her, she pulled the
wrap tighter around her body. How long had he been
watching her sleep? The question made her shiver
violently.

'What the hell are you doing in my room?' she
demanded, her green eyes flashing. 'Get out and leave
me alone!'

His mouth tightened ominously as he gazed down at her.

'I've brought your suitcases up,' he answered dispassionately. 'I thought you might need them. I knocked, there was no answer—I thought you might be ill.' His voice was cold and polite, betrayed by the anger in his eyes.

'You needn't have bothered,' Fay retorted ungratefully, attack being her only form of defence against the unexpected and shocking weakness spreading rapidly through her limbs, at the sight of him, so strong and so attractive, as he towered over her.

'Get out of here!'

Before she could say anything more, his arms had shot out and grabbed her mercilessly, pulling her to her feet in one rough movement.

'You need a lesson in manners,' he grated harshly, shaking her slightly, his strong brown fingers digging into her soft flesh, bruising her.

'Not from you!' she hissed furiously, struggling in his grasp. He smiled slightly.

'From me,' he murmured softly, dangerously as he lowered his dark head towards her.

Fay stopped struggling immediately, hypnotised by his nearness, the clean male smell of him, and the silver glitter of his eyes beneath their heavy lids. She would not fight him—she would show him that he could not affect her, or intimidate her in any way.

His mouth found hers slowly, fiercely, and his kiss was devastating. He forced her lips apart with anger and expertise, and as soon as he felt her response—a response that she could not hold back despite herself, despite every ounce of will-power inside her—his lips became gentle and sensual. He explored the sweetness of her mouth thoroughly, deeply and so slowly, his hands releasing her arms to cup her face gently.

Forgetting her anger and outrage, forgetting everything but the pleasure of his mouth, Fay put her arms up around his neck, her fingers tangling in the dark thickness of his hair, unwilling to let him go. Desire was flooding through her, desire she had never felt before for any man, as his hard mouth moved across her face, caressing her eyes, her cheeks, her forehead, slowly, hungrily, and with a jolting shock that brought her back to her senses she realised that she wanted that mouth on her body.

'Gabriel. . . .' she whispered softly, wanting to say something but not knowing what.

He lifted his head reluctantly and looked at her, his eyes almost black, heavy with desire, and his hands dropped from her face, leaving her alone, bereft and strangely cold. They stood for a moment, almost touching, watching each other, both knowing the inevitability of what had happened between them. Gabriel smiled and lifting his hand, touched her mouth gently.

'That's better,' he said wickedly. 'No anger.'

He turned away and strolled towards the door. 'Dinner is at eight,' he said softly, and left the room.

Fay stood still and shocked for long moments after he had gone, then with a great effort of will, she pulled herself together. She felt suddenly disgusted with herself for responding with such abandon in his arms. She did not know him, and had only just freed herself from one unsatisfactory relationship. She had no intention of falling into another one, so soon. Try as she might, she could not picture Sam's face in her mind. It was already filled to the exclusion of all else with disturbing grey eyes and a strong sensual mouth.

She shook her head angrily, as if to dislodge these images, and then remembered his parting words: 'Dinner is at eight.' That meant he would be staying.

Was there to be no escape? she wondered despairingly as she began to collect things for her shower. It was nearly seven, she had slept for two hours, and she did not have much time. She unpacked her cases quickly, then made her way to the bathroom. Her shower was hot and soothing, and she shampood her hair vigorously, glad to be rid of the dirt of travelling. After the shower, she slipped on the wrap and made her way hurriedly back to her bedroom. She dried her hair quickly with the portable hairdryer she had brought with her, then turned her attention to her face. She stared at her reflection in the mirror for a moment. Rich and shiny auburn hair fell to her shoulders, and framed her pale heart-shaped face—all fragile hollows, since her illness, emerald eyes—her best feature, huge and fringed with thick lashes, a fairly ordinary nose and a full soft mouth. She was aware that she was attractive, but she certainly was not beautiful, she thought wryly.

Sighing, she began to apply her make-up. She applied her eye make-up carefully, using a little more than usual, trying to pretend to herself that it was not for Gabriel Winter's benefit, and failing miserably. She coloured her mouth carefully with rich colour, then brushed out her unmanageable hair. Satisfied, she turned her attention to what she would wear.

Sophie always dressed for dinner, a tradition she was unwilling to let go of, and Fay chose her dress carefully. She finally decided on a black crêpe-de-chine, simply cut, with a high neck and long sleeves. It was very plain, but she knew that she looked good in it. It clung to her curved and lissom body perfectly, even though she had lost a little weight.

The final touch was a gold brooch, which had been her grandmother's, and large gold hoops swinging from her ears. Looking at herself in a full-length mirror inside one of the wardrobes, she was well satisfied with her stunning reflection.

Checking her watch, she saw it was seven-fifty, and stepping into high-heeled black shoes, she switched off the bedroom light and made her way downstairs, trying to ignore the trembling feeling in her stomach at the thought of seeing Gabriel Winter again.

She entered the lounge nervously, only to find it empty. Somewhat relieved, she made her way over to the tray of drinks on top of a tall oak cabinet and poured herself a small sherry. She sipped it quickly, hoping that it would quell some of the fluttering nerves inside her. It did not work. She jumped visibly when her aunt entered the room.

'Ah, Fay—I'm glad you've helped yourself to a drink. You look lovely, my dear.'

'Thank you. Can I get you a drink?' Fay asked, smiling at her aunt.

'I'll have a small sherry—dry. We must have a long chat, Fay, I want to hear all the news.'

'Yes——' Fay turned from her task of pouring a sherry for her aunt. 'I wanted to ask you, Sophie, about Gabriel Winter. . . .' Her voice trailed off with horror as she saw him entering the room. She turned away, but not before their eyes had met for a brief second and she knew that he was amused by the question he was not supposed to have heard.

'Now that I'm here, you can ask me in person,' he drawled slowly, amusement still apparent in his voice.

Fay's heart began to hammer wildly, but luckily Sophie intervened.

'Now, Gabe,' she scolded, 'don't tease the poor child. What will you have to drink?'

Gabriel laughed deep in his throat. 'You win, Sophie, and I'll have a Scotch—straight.'

'Will you get it, Fay, while you're there?'

'Of course.' Trying to control her shaking hands,

Fay poured out a measure of Scotch.

She handed Sophie her sherry, then keeping her eyes firmly down she passed the whisky to Gabriel. Their hands touched and Fay flinched away from the contact, as Gabriel murmured his sardonic thanks.

Then she was safe, as she made her way over to the other side of the room to retrieve her own drink—a drink she sorely needed, after the events of the last few minutes.

She avoided most of the conversation over dinner. Sophie was obviously concerned at her silence, so she pleaded a slight headache. This was untrue, of course, but she could not let her aunt know the truth, it was too ridiculous. She was deeply affected by the tall, proud and attractive man seated opposite her at the table. She glanced at him now, as he chatted to Sophie. He looked devastatingly handsome tonight, in a black velvet jacket and a white shirt that accentuated the tan of his skin. His eyes were veiled, faintly amused, and he was gracefully relaxed, witty and charming. Even to glance at him made her stomach lurch sickeningly.

The meal was absolutely delicious—Sophie's housekeeper, Mrs Bond, was a superb cook, but Fay could not do justice to it, so disturbed was she. After a few choking mouthfuls of creamy soup, she pushed her bowl away and pushed the tender lamb and vegetables around her plate so much that even Sophie noticed.

'Fay, are you feeling unwell? You've hardly touched your food. Is your headache very bad?' she asked with concern.

Fay smiled weakly, supremely aware of Gabriel's grey glance suddenly intent on her.

'I . . . I'm sorry, Sophie. The meal is lovely—I'm just not hungry—it must be all the travelling—I'm sorry,' she said haltingly.

'Don't apologise, my dear, it's not your fault. You're

still not fully recovered from your illness—and you can't rush these things.'

'You've been ill?' Gabriel's deep attractive voice cut into their conversation. Fay looked at him, his eyes were dark and brooding as they rested on her flushed face.

'Yes, I've had pneumonia—but I'm better now, really! It's just the journey—I'm easily tired at the moment. . . .' She stopped abruptly, aware that she was rambling. 'Sophie, would you excuse me? I think I'd better go to bed.' She got to her feet shakily.

Her aunt nodded. 'Of course, my dear. I'll bring you up a cup of tea.'

'Thank you.' Fay leaned over and kissed her aunt's cheek affectionately. 'Goodnight, Sophie—Mr Winter.' Without waiting for any reply, she walked from the room, trying to ignore the grey eyes that followed her, and made her way upstairs wearily. At least it was over, and with luck she would not see Gabriel Winter again.

Pushing thoughts of him from her mind, she washed and undressed, finding the effort of climbing into bed almost too much for her. Once in bed, however, she felt wide awake and thoughts of the man downstairs crept back, unwanted, into her mind.

A knock on the door roused her from her reverie. It was her aunt with the promised cup of tea, and Fay sat up, reaching for it eagerly.

'Thanks, Sophie, just what I need.' She smiled. 'I am sorry about dinner.'

'It doesn't matter,' her aunt cut in. 'You did come here to rest, and that's what you'll do.'

Fay sipped her tea gratefully, and Sophie looked at her thoughtfully.

'What do you think of Gabe?' she asked suddenly.

There was silence for a moment.

'He's very attractive, I suppose,' Fay managed at last, hoping that she was not giving anything away. 'You're good friends?'

'Yes—I'm very fond of him. He's a good man, I hope you and he will get on,' her aunt replied.

Fay shrugged, doubting this very much. 'Does he live near?' she asked casually.

Sophie laughed merrily, and Fay stared at her, perplexed.

'He lives here—didn't I mention it in my letter? I'm getting absentminded in my old age,' Sophie shook her head. 'He's renting the top floor—you remember, your uncle had it converted into a flat for Judy and her husband. Ah, it was such a pity about their marriage—mind you, I have to say it, even though she's my own daughter, Arthur spoiled her something wicked——' She paused. 'What was I saying? Oh yes—it's quite self-contained up there, but Gabe comes down for meals, it's more convenient for Mrs Bond, and I enjoy his company, I must admit. He's an interesting man. Have you read any of his books?'

Fay, who had been staring at her aunt, shocked and open-mouthed, now shook her head. Of course! No wonder his name had seemed familiar—he was quite a famous writer, many of his books were best-sellers.

'No, I haven't read any of his books,' she replied finally, and rather breathlessly.

'Well, you must,' her aunt said firmly. 'They're extremely good.' She stared at Fay, noticing her silence, and mistaking her shock for weariness.

'I'm sorry, my dear, for chattering on when you're so tired. Once I get started—well, you know!' She stood up. 'We'll talk tomorrow, you must get some sleep now. Goodnight.' Leaning over she kissed her niece's cheek gently.

'Goodnight, Sophie. It's so nice to be staying with

you again,' Fay smiled.

Her aunt left the room and Fay was left alone with her thoughts, as she settled back into bed and switched off the lights. So Gabriel Winter was staying here. She smiled to herself—so much for never seeing him again, although she had to admit now that in a secret way she was glad. He intrigued her, attracted her, disturbed her, and she would have to come to terms with her feelings. It had been a long, strange day, and still bemused, she fell asleep. Her dreams warm and soft, dreams of a man with clear grey eyes, and a mouth that promised heaven.

CHAPTER TWO

Fay woke early the next morning, feeling refreshed and wide awake. She had slept deeply, soundly, better than she had done for months. She climbed out of bed, disregarding the cold, and went over to the window to look out. The sun was bright and weak, sparkling dazzlingly on the snow that lay deep and undisturbed. There was nothing but snow for miles around, and opening the window, she drew deep breaths of the clear crisp morning air.

She smiled to herself, suddenly glad to be alive. She would become strong here, she thought happily; the fresh clean air would heal her body, and the sheer beauty of the place would soothe her mind.

She turned from the window, hearing a light tap on the door.

'Come in, Sophie,' she called as the door opened.

But it was not Sophie who entered but Gabriel Winter with a tray in his hands. He looked lean and attractive in tight denim jeans, the faded material moulding his strong legs, and a black, round-necked sweater, and Fay felt practically undressed in her thin silk nightdress. His eyes slid over her slowly, veiled and unreadable in the clear morning light. Then he smiled.

'Your breakfast,' he said, indicating the tray. 'Sophie thought you might be tired this morning.'

Fay stared at him suspiciously, unable to stop the hammering of her heart at the sight of him, so tall and virile as he stood before her.

'*You* didn't have to bring it up,' she said nastily, the

words spoken before she realised it.

The smile died abruptly in Gabriel's eyes, and his mouth tightened. When he spoke, however, his voice was dispassionate.

'Sophie trusts me,' he stated significantly. He turned to go, and Fay realised with a leaping of her heart that she did not want him to go, not now, not ever. She ran to him, touching his arm shyly, as he reached the door.

'I'm sorry,' she said breathlessly, 'I didn't mean to be so rude. Thank you for bringing the tray.'

Gabriel stared down at her for a moment, his eyes darkening disturbingly as they rested on her mouth. He shrugged lazily, this action drawing her glance to his broad and powerful shoulders.

'Forget it,' he murmured softly, and something in his voice brought her eyes back to his face, and her mouth went dry as she caught his expression.

'You're very beautiful—but you know that, don't you?' he said, tilting her chin with strong fingers, forcing her to meet his stormy grey eyes.

Fay shook her head wordlessly, and if he was going to say anything else, he changed his mind, and releasing her chin abruptly, he turned on his heel and strode from the room.

Fay stared at the closed door, her heart still pounding. She was no match for this man. Sighing, she picked up the tray and sat down on the bed, feeling hungry. There was boiled eggs and toast, jam and coffee, and she ate everything, finishing with three cups of strong black coffee.

Feeling a great deal better, she showered quickly and dressed, in olive-green corduroy trousers and a thick olive-green sweater. Then, leaving her face bare of make-up, she brushed out her thick, unruly hair and made her way downstairs.

She found her aunt in the lounge, reading the newspaper in front of the fire.

'Good morning, Sophie. Thanks for sending my breakfast up—it was a lovely thought.' Fay greeted her with a kiss.

Sophie smiled cheerfully. 'I didn't know if you'd be well enough to get up for breakfast—I see I was wrong. You look wonderful, my dear.'

'I feel wonderful,' Fay replied, 'and you must promise not to worry about me, Sophie. I'm not ill—in fact I thought I'd go for a walk this morning, it's such a lovely day.'

Her aunt nodded. 'That's a good idea. I'll ask Gabe to show you round, it's some years since you've stayed here, and things have changed.'

'No, really, don't bother asking ... er ... Mr Winter. I'd rather go alone,' Fay cut in hastily. The last thing she wanted was a walk with Gabriel Winter.

Sophie stared at her curiously, noticing the sudden betraying colour in her niece's cheeks.

'You must go alone, if you prefer to,' was all she said. Then, 'But before you do go, Fay, tell me all the news from London—I'm bursting with curiosity!'

Laughing, Fay took a seat opposite her aunt, and the next hour was pleasantly spent, recounting all the news from home. Not that there was much actual news, but Sophie wanted to know all about her job, her flat, her parents, Sam, and all the plays and films Fay had seen lately.

Fay started at the beginning, explaining about her job, as assistant, secretary and general dogsbody to an up-and-coming young film director. It was interesting work, and she enjoyed it immensely. Paul, her boss, had given her unlimited time off to get over her illness, probably because he felt guilty about it, she explained wryly to Sophie. She had contracted pneumonia while out on location with Paul in the wilds of Scotland, and although she did not blame him at all for the series of disasters that had started her illness, she knew that he felt responsible.

She also told Sophie about her new flat, near the centre of London, which she had been very lucky to get, and her aunt wanted all the details of colour-schemes, furniture, and neighbours.

News about her parents and Sam came next, and Fay could not help disclosing the fact that she was very worried about her relationship with Sam. She explained what had happened, and Sophie listened sympathetically to her fears and worries, assuring her that she must stay in Yorkshire as long as she liked, until she had things clear in her mind.

Finally they were interrupted by Mrs Bond, coming in with a tray of mid-morning coffee. Fay enthused honestly, over the previous night's meal, explaining why she had eaten so little, and was rewarded with the housekeeper's sweet smile. Mrs Bond had been at Lambrigg House for many years, and she and Sophie were very close. Fay did not want to upset her in any way.

Sophie was pouring out coffee for them both when Gabriel Winter strolled indolently into the room.

'Ah, I thought I could smell Mrs Bond's excellent coffee,' he smiled at Sophie.

She beamed at him. 'Sit down, Gabe, I'll pour you a cup. Not working today?'

He eased his long frame into a chair, and lit a cigarette before replying.

'No, I'm too restless,' he said, his eyes enigmatic as they rested on Fay.

Sophie followed the direction of his gaze.

'Fay will be going out for a walk after coffee. Perhaps you could show her round?'

Fay heard his low agreement with a sinking heart.

What was Sophie up to now, she thought irritably—matchmaking? She could not stay angry for long, however. Her aunt was so sweet, so slyly innocent as she smiled roguishly at them both.

'That's settled, then,' she said firmly. Fay shook her head with exasperation and grinned back.

'Fay's been telling me all the news from London,' Sophie said, turning her attention to Gabriel. He smiled, drawing deeply on his cigarette, his eyes mocking as they met Fay's.

Her coffee finished, she got to her feet hurriedly, breaking the contact between them.

'I'll go and get my coat and boots,' she said to Sophie, by way of an excuse.

'Ten minutes,' Gabriel drawled. 'I'll see you outside.'

Without answering, Fay left the room and ran upstairs. She would not be manipulated, even for Sophie. She would not walk with Gabriel Winter, she would be long gone in ten minutes.

She glanced at herself in the mirror—at least some of the colour was returning to her face. She still had dark shadows beneath her eyes, and the weight loss from her face had pronounced her cheekbones, leaving her face hollow and fragile. Unknown to her, it gave her a poignant, haunting beauty, a mysterious defenceless look. She grimaced at her reflection. There was no time to put on any make-up, she thought grimly, pulling on her boots and grabbing her coat and gloves.

She made her way downstairs quickly, creeping past the lounge, where she could hear Gabriel Winter's low seductive laughter. Shivering involuntarily, she opened the huge front door carefully and stepped outside, pulling it closed as quietly as she could.

She crossed the drive and began walking through the trees that surrounded the house, seeking cover. It was a beautiful day—freezing cold, but so fresh and bright that Fay felt exhilarated, as she tramped through the snow that came up over her ankles with every step. She also felt profoundly relieved that she had escaped Gabriel Winter—it was good to be alone, even though her thoughts were filled with him.

Making her way over the wooded hillock behind the house, she came to her favourite haunt as a child a small, now frozen waterfall, cutting its way down the other side of the hill to the river beyond. She stopped, short of breath, and gazed up at the sky. High thin white clouds grazed the blue—more snow on the way, she remembered with a smile. Perhaps they would be snowed in—even at twenty-five, she found the prospect childishly exciting, and she laughed out loud, as her bright gaze scanned the horizon. At that second she saw the tall, well-remembered figure of a man standing at the top of the hill, and the laughter died on her lips. He was watching her, intruding on her solitude, and although he was still quite a few yards away, she could clearly distinguish the anger on his face.

Fay turned on her heel and began retracing her steps down the hill, her pleasure gone, only wanting to be back at the house. She heard him behind her and picked up speed, but she was no match for his tall striding movements, especially in the snow. She felt his restraining hand on her arm with inevitability and dread. She might have known that he would find her, it had been too easy to get away. She turned to face him with a strange defeated anger.

Looking defiantly into his lean angry face, she experienced the usual shock and quickening of her heartbeat that always accompanied the sight of him, and sighed. He looked hard and sure of himself, and devastatingly attractive in the weak morning sunlight, and she bowed her head before all this, defeatedly waiting for him to speak first, waiting for his anger to wash over her.

'Why didn't you wait?' he asked harshly, angrily, his grip on her arm tightening painfully.

'I didn't want to walk with you,' Fay answered honestly, staring up at him challengingly, her breath catching in her throat at the unsmiling glitter of his narrowed eyes.

'Why are you always so damned unpleasant?' he muttered through clenched teeth, and shook her, making her cry out with pain, pain that made her lose her temper, as she tried to prise his steel-strong fingers from her arm with no success.

'What makes you think that you're so irresistible?' she shouted back at him, angrily fighting the threatening weakness that his nearness induced. 'I can tell you—you're not. I hate you! Let me go!'

With her free hand she began to hit him wildly, raining blows on his chest and shoulders. Gabriel's mouth twisted cruelly, as he easily caught her other hand and twisted both her arms behind her back, leaving her defenceless, at his mercy. Fay stared up at him with wide emerald eyes, her anger gone, replaced with a dizzying mixture of fear and desire. She had really gone too far this time. A hard muscle was jerking spasmodically in his jaw, his strong face was a taut, still mask of anger, his eyes dark and dangerous beneath heavy lids.

He arched her closer to him, until their faces were only inches apart, and she could feel his warm breath on her mouth, her own breath coming in sharp, uneven gasps.

'Damn you, Fay, you provoke me,' he grated savagely.

'Go to hell!' she whispered weakly, goading him, the words parting her lips as he lowered his head slowly, so very slowly that she could hardly bear it. Intolerable need swayed her towards him, uncaring of the pain she caused in her arms.

His mouth touched hers like an explosion. He was punishing her, but he was hungry for her too, and her desire responded. With a hoarse groan, he put his arms around her, sliding beneath the heavy fur of her coat, and they clung together, alone, in the snow. She heard him murmur her name as his tongue traced the bruised and responsive outline of her lips, before possessing them once again, with devastating mastery. Achingly, she slid her hands to his shoulders, delighting in the tightening of the powerful muscles beneath her fingers, and arching back her head, she shuddered as his cruel, sensual mouth tantalisingly brushed the softness of her white throat.

The knowledge that he was as deeply aroused as herself made her head spin weakly with need for him. His strong, lean fingers beneath her coat were moulding her caressingly to him, and she wanted him to lay her down and make love to her. He would love her fully, expertly and sweetly—he would teach her to please him, and God help her, she wanted to. Never before had a man made her feel this way—not even Sam, and she might have married him.

These humiliating thoughts brought her sickly back to her senses. Her fingers fell from Gabriel's broad shoulders immediately, and she wrenched herself from his arms, leaving a little of her heart behind, and trying to control her traitorous body.

She glanced up at the man standing before her, and her stomach turned over. She had to find some defence against the feelings he so carelessly aroused in her. How could she keep him away from her? Gabriel was breathing deeply, his eyes lazy and slumbrous, but he made no attempt to take her back into his arms. Was he waiting for her to fling herself back at him? She had to attack.

'How dare you!' she accused him furiously. 'Don't ever touch me again. I'm engaged to be married. My fiancé will kill you, if he ever finds out what you've done!' This lie was the first thing that came into her mind, and it seemed to work, because even as she watched, a bleak, cynical look shuttered the hungry desire in his eyes, and they became as cold as the ice beneath his feet. His glance slid to her wedding finger, and he smiled bitterly, coldly.

'If you were mine, you'd wear my ring. You wouldn't look at another man,' he stated in a brutally soft voice.

Guilt, and a nagging regret that she had lied to him, and let him think so badly of her, made Fay retort heatedly:

'But I'm not yours—I never shall be!' Damn her voice for trembling so much, for making a liar of her.

Gabriel shrugged idly, his eyes still bleak and remote.

'Are you so sure?' he taunted cynically, his eyes boring into her very soul, making her head drop shamefully. 'I think not, Fay. When I want you, I shall have you, and you will never deny me.'

He laughed mirthlessly. 'And yet you intend to go to another man, knowing this—are you so dishonest with yourself?'

Confused, Fay shook her head. She had lied to him to protect herself, and now he was turning it back on her. She had read in the newspapers of his casual affairs—he desired but did not love. She would never be just another of his conquests, but she had no defence against him. She burst into flames every time he touched her—her lies would keep him away from her, they were her only chance. Tears of self-pity and frustration gathered in her eyes, threatening to overflow down her pale cheeks.

'No . . . yes . . . oh, I don't know! Why are you doing this to me?' she whispered desperately, her beautiful eyes pleading with him.

Gabriel sighed, running his hand wearily around the back of his neck, his anger gone.

'Because you want me to take the responsibility for your desires, because I want you—you know that, and the thought of you in another man's arms is driving me crazy—oh, what the hell!' He turned away, cursing savagely, reaching for his cigarettes.

Fay stared at him curiously. He was a strange man, honest and intriguing, and she wished with all her heart suddenly that she had not lied to him. But it was too late to take it back and it was her only defence against him. She could not deny that there was a strong attraction between them, an attraction that she could not resist, however hard she tried. She pressed a trembling hand to her stomach, where desire was still shivering inside her. What would she do? Was she ready for another relationship so soon? Perhaps there was only one way to find out.

'Kiss me, Gabriel,' she said clearly, shocked by her own words, her heart pounding at the implication of them. She saw him stiffen, and heard the swift intake of his breath, but he did not turn around to face her.

'Gabriel——' she repeated softly.

'I heard you,' he said thickly, turning suddenly to watch her with tormented eyes. 'What perverse game are you playing now, Fay?'

She flinched from the harshness in his voice, but answered readily.

'You were right, I am being dishonest with myself. I want you to kiss me again. . . .' She swallowed ner-

vously, her voice trailing off weakly at the expression
on his dark, proud face.

She had not meant to say any of this to him, but
there was something about this strange, powerful man
that demanded her honesty, even as she lied to him.
Was she already a little in love with him? She knew
the answer with a sudden and depressing flash of insight, realising that whatever she did feel for Gabriel
Winter she would never feel for any man again in her
lifetime.

Gabriel sighed heavily, a betraying muscle jerking
frantically in his jaw.

'No, Fay, you don't know what you're asking,' he
finally replied, in a low, carefully controlled voice. He
pushed away the hand she had laid tentatively on his
arm. 'No,' he repeated harshly.

Sick with shame at his rejection, Fay turned on her
heel and began to make her way down the hill towards
the house. She had made an utter fool of herself—how
he would laugh at her! she thought bitterly. He had
demanded her honesty, honesty that had been difficult
to give, then he had rejected her. Good heavens, she
admonished herself angrily, what was the matter with
her? She had only known this man for two days and
already he had turned her life and her emotions upside
down. Today they were enemies, and she did not want
that. It would upset Sophie and it would be very difficult, both under the same roof, meals, evenings spent
together. Something had to be done.

'Fay, wait . . .!' With a few long strides, Gabriel
caught up with her and was beside her, his hands thrust
deep into his pockets. She glanced at him covertly and
sighed deep inside. His face was fast becoming the only
face in the world for her, and she had to do something—maybe make it right between them. She
stopped walking and turned towards him, looking ap-

prehensively into his face.

'Gabriel, can we start again? Forget the bad things and be friends?' she asked, smiling gently at him, suddenly filled with confidence.

He stared down at her, and she saw the warmth and the light in his suddenly clear grey eyes.

'Do you think we can make it as friends?' he asked, returning her smile.

'I don't know,' she replied honestly, 'but we can try—yes, I think we can be friends.'

Gabriel opened his arms, and she went into them joyfully. He held her tightly for a few moments and she tried to ignore the devastating effect this had on her. It was so good to be near him, without conflict. If she could have these strong arms around her for ever, it would be too short a time.

He looked down at her, a smile curving his firm mouth.

'We've started again,' he murmured, pressing his mouth gently to her forehead before releasing her. A bubble of happiness rose up inside her.

'Yes. Can we go for our walk now?' she asked happily.

'Of course—come on!'

He took her hand and they began walking back up the hill, to the frozen waterfall. The sky had darkened, and heavy snow began to fall again as they walked. Fay smiled up at Gabriel, her green eyes brilliant.

'Can I ask you some questions?' Gabriel nodded. 'How old are you?' She gazed up at him guilelessly as she spoke, and he laughed out loud.

'Thirty-six,' he replied amusedly, all the strain gone from his face, leaving him relaxed and extremely attractive, to Fay's searching glance.

'I'm twenty-five,' she volunteered candidly. 'You're very brown, have you been abroad?'

'I was living in Sicily until last year,' he answered, still smiling at her.

'Oh.' Fay digested this information carefully, storing it away in her mind. 'How long have you been here with Sophie?'

'About four months. I needed some peace—needed to get away for a while.' He was remote again, his eyes bleak and troubled.

'Let's build a snowman,' Fay suggested extravagantly, wanting to take his mind off whatever pained him. 'When I was a little girl I used to come and stay here in the holidays, and Judy—that's my cousin—and I used to build a snowman on top of this hill every year. I bet you haven't built a snowman for years and years!' she teased.

Gabriel laughed again, a low, husky chuckle.

'That's very true,' he replied, mocking himself with good humour.

They built a huge snowman on top of the hill, talking the whole while, and Fay began to get to know him. She found out that he was not married, about the vast amount of travelling he had done, about his books, and about him as a person. In turn she told him about her illness, her job and Sam, although it had to be admitted that she could not bring herself to tell him much about Sam. She wanted to tell him the truth, that she was not engaged, but somehow she could not—the words stuck in her throat, a deceit between them.

Gabriel listened to her carefully, watching her animated face intently, with traces of his desire for her still darkening his eyes.

Finally the snowman was finished, and both of them were covered with snow from the steady downpour that showed no signs of letting up.

'I'm starving! It must be lunchtime,' Fay laughed breathlessly.

Gabriel glanced at his watch.

'It's after one, so it must indeed be lunchtime,' he agreed smilingly. He took her hand, and they trudged down the hill, and back to the house talking and laughing like happy children all the way, their friendship temporarily sealed.

CHAPTER THREE

LATER that afternoon Fay took a long, hot bath and relaxing in the soft scented water, she reflected on the day's events. Lunch had been the first meal she had really enjoyed since arriving at Lambrigg House. It had been happy and relaxed, the tension and strain between Gabriel and herself gone, and she had allowed herself the bitter-sweet pleasure of gazing at him openly as they ate. She had committed to memory every detail of his face, the angular bone structure, the movements of his strong, sensual mouth as he talked and the disturbing colour changes of his eyes whenever he looked at her.

Even Sophie had noticed the change of atmosphere between them and had eyed them both speculatively during the meal.

Fay scrubbed her back languidly, pondering on the strange relationship developing between them. She had never before encountered a man like Gabriel Winter, and it was a heady experience. He affected her deeply, just how deeply she was not yet sure, and it worried her a little. She was afraid that she would become more involved than he would. He wanted her, Fay knew, but she felt sure that his feelings ended there. At least they were friends for the moment, she concluded, shampooing her hair vigorously and deciding not to think about it.

After lunch, Sophie had taken her customary nap and Gabriel had gone upstairs to work, leaving Fay alone. She had sat by the fire for a while, glancing through Sophie's numerous photograph albums, with pleasure and a great many memories, pictures of herself as a little girl, grubby and defiant, made her smile. As an only child she had looked forward eagerly to holidays spent with Sophie and her two cousins Judy and Lee, here in the wilds of Yorkshire, and what happy times they had had.

Still reminiscing, Fay had finally put the albums aside and had begun a letter to her parents. In the letter, with great difficulty, she told them of her break-up with Sam. They would be disappointed and upset, she knew, but they had to know the truth. She also wrote about Sophie, Gabriel and the snowman they had built, not going into much detail about Gabriel, or the various incidents that had taken place between them. She did not even like to think about those, let alone write them down. Then sealing up her letter and leaving it for Mrs Bond to post on her way home, Fay had succumbed to the tiredness invading her limbs and had made her way upstairs for a nap.

Stepping out of the bath now, she wrapped herself in a huge thick towel and began drying herself. She felt alert and refreshed; it was so good to get away from London and her usual hectic routine. This place was working its magic already. Smiling to herself, she dried her hair quickly and put on a light make-up before dressing. She chose a green silk dress for dinner. It was the exact colour of her eyes and its loose, buttoned style hinted at the curves beneath even as it hid her slight weight loss. It flared out just below the knee, and was hemmed with embroidery in contrasting colours. She slipped it on quickly and, satisfied with her appearance, left the bedroom.

She met Gabriel on the landing looking dark and disturbing in a grey velvet dinner jacket and slim-fitting dark trousers. Fay smiled at him nervously.

'You look beautiful,' he murmured huskily, his eyes narrowing as they appraised her thoroughly, sliding darkly over her like a caress. He took her arm and they made their way down the stairs together. At such close proximity she could smell the faint masculine scent of his after-shave and it went to her head like strong wine. He was going out for dinner, and ridiculously Fay realised that she would miss him. She wondered if his dinner date was with a woman. Dear God, she was jealous! She longed to ask him, needing his reassurance, but could not—it was none of her business.

They reached the lounge, far too soon for Fay's liking, where Sophie was sitting by the fire sipping a small pre-dinner sherry. She stood up as they entered the room, eyeing them both as they stood close together—the perfect couple.

'Ah—Fay, Gabriel. Have you time for a quick drink before you go?' she asked him.

He glanced at his watch. 'I think not, Sophie,' he answered, his regretful eyes on Fay's shining head.

'Well, drive carefully, it's getting worse out there,' she smiled.

He left the room gracefully with Fay's discreet eyes following him all the way, only coming to her senses when her aunt pressed a glass into her hand.

'I'm so glad that you two seem to be getting on now,' she remarked, watching Fay carefully.

'Yes—we're friends now, I think. Do you know where he's gone tonight?' Fay asked, trying to sound casual.

Sophie smiled. 'Yes, I believe he's gone to the Baxters' for dinner. They've got an enormous house about twelve miles from here. I don't think you know them, do you?'

'No, I don't think so, the name is unfamiliar,' Fay

replied, wondering how she could get more information from Sophie without revealing her jealousy or her particular interest. 'Has he known them long?'

Sophie flashed her a wise look and continued:

'Gabe and John Baxter have been friends for many years. John's a good deal older than Gabe, though, and I do know that his daughter Lucy—dreadful creature!—is more than a little interested in Gabe, she's been here for dinner a number of times, with John, of course, and she wasn't exactly subtle.' She stopped, seeing Fay's suddenly miserable face. 'I shouldn't worry, my dear, I'm sure he doesn't feel anything for her, not in that way.'

Fay tried to smile unsuccessfully.

'Why should I mind? It's none of my business anyway,' she lied. Then, 'Oh, Sophie, I'm so confused! He's hit me like a bombshell. I can't even look at him without wanting him. What shall I do?' She stared at her aunt with tormented eyes, unable to keep up her charade of not caring any longer.

Sophie squeezed her arm reassuringly. 'Don't upset yourself, Fay, it will work itself out, this thing between you and Gabriel, if you let it. I've seen the way he looks at you—I wish I was thirty years younger! Just be honest with yourself.'

Fay smiled sadly. 'That's what he said, but I'm still afraid. I know I could love him, but I don't want to make a fool of myself again.' She sighed heavily. 'I'm sorry for burdening you with all this. . . .'

'Don't apologise, my dear. But I don't know what to say to you. I can't advise you. Gabriel is a good man—he'll be honest with you, I'm sure.'

'I know—please don't worry. I wrote to Mum and Dad this afternoon and told them about Sam, at least I was honest with him even if I can't be honest with myself. Oh, let's go in for dinner!' They walked into the dining room arm in arm with Fay determined not to spoil Sophie's meal. There was nothing more to say, and Fay was glad that she had confided in her aunt. At least she could laugh at her own self-pity for the moment.

The evening passed pleasantly. Fay heard all the rest of Sophie's news, and after their delicious meal they sat in front of the fire and listened to the radio—a play that Sophie particularly wanted to hear. Life moved at a gentle pace here, and Fay felt happy and content having successfully pushed her worry about Gabriel to the back of her mind.

A little after eleven, Sophie retired to bed, and Fay sat alone with her thoughts in front of the dying fire. She still felt wide awake and alert. The nap she had taken that afternoon had left her refreshed, and she would not be able to sleep for some hours yet, and it was so warm and comfortable by the fire. She switched off all the lights except a small glass lamp on the mantelpiece and pulled open the heavy velvet curtains. It was still snowing and she moved back to her comfortable chair to watch. She told herself sternly that she was not waiting up for Gabriel; that would be too ridiculous, it was just too early to go to bed.

She watched the snow until she felt almost hypnotised, and was so deep in thought that she did not hear the front door closing or the subdued footsteps across the lounge until he was standing in front of her, staring down at her with questioning eyes, his jacket casually hooked over his shoulder.

'Are you all right?'

She looked up at him blankly for a second before replying.

'I'm sorry, I was miles away.'

Gabriel smiled slightly. 'I need a drink, would you like one?'

'A brandy would be lovely, thanks,' Fay answered, watching his broad back intently as he poured the drinks. He looked very tired and there was a tense, strained rigidity about his spine.

'Are the roads any worse?' she asked, not really interested, but unable to bear the silence that was stretching between them, wishing that she had gone up to her room before he had come in.

Gabriel nodded. 'A couple more days like this and I reckon we could be snowed in.' He handed her a glass, then sat down on the couch opposite to her. He had loosened his tie and unbuttoned his shirt at the throat, and his strength and virility were potently evident as he sat just a couple of feet away, his face lean and heavily shadowed in the dim light. He lit a cigarette wearily and drew the smoke deep into his lungs.

'Lord, I'm tired!' he muttered, throwing back his drink in one mouthful.

'You look it,' Fay replied wickedly. 'How long is it since you slept?'

Gabriel shrugged gracefully, tiredly. 'Two days, maybe,' he answered carelessly, stubbing out his cigarette.

'Is something worrying you?' Fay felt an overpowering need to help him, which was quite ridiculous, she told herself. A man like Gabriel Winter would never need her help.

He smiled, his eyes enigmatic.

'Are you going to sort out my problems for me, Fay?' he asked softly, and Fay dropped her eyes, her hands twisting nervously in her lap, feeling well and truly out of her depth.

When she finally lifted her head, he was leaning his dark head back against the softness of the couch, his eyes closed. She watched him for a moment before getting quietly to her feet, intending to leave the room and go to bed. But almost against her will, drawn by something deep inside her that would not be denied, she found herself behind him, staring down at his dark head, and of their own volition her hands slid slowly on to his broad shoulders as she began to massage the tense knotted muscles beneath her fingers. She could feel the warmth of his skin through the thin cotton of his shirt, and just to touch him made her heart beat painfully fast and excitement flutter in her stomach.

The collar of his shirt prevented her from massaging the rigid muscles of his neck, and as he had not moved, or opened his eyes since she had begun, she assumed that he was asleep and her desire to give him some relief overcame her timidity and embarrassment as she began to undo the top buttons of his shirt, carefully, so as not to disturb or waken him. This done without incident, she slid her hands beneath the thin material and began to expertly knead his neck and shoulders again.

She could feel some of the tension draining from him as she worked, and the pleasure this gave her was incredible. His skin was smooth and warm, stretched tautly over the powerful muscles of his shoulders, wonderful to her sensitive fingertips.

Suddenly Gabriel breathed in deeply. 'Mmm, that's good,' he murmured huskily.

Fay's hands froze immediately, embarrassment paralysing her. 'I . . . I'm sorry, I thought you were . . . asleep,' she stammered, thankful that her furious blushing could not be seen in the darkness.

'Don't stop,' he commanded softly. And obeying him instinctively, Fay began moving her hands over his skin again, falteringly. The fact that he was aware of her stroking, soothing fingers and that his breathing had become deeper only served to heighten the shivering desire that the mere touch of his bare skin had awakened in her, and her hands slowly began to stroke lower over the beginnings of the crisp dark hair that matted his broad chest. Timid at first, she became bolder until his hands reached up and closed over hers, imprisoning them against the warm hard wall of his body. He groaned her name and with fast, sure movements, pulled her into his arms.

'Do you know what you're doing to me?' he whispered softly, his strong arms like bands of steel, his hard mouth only inches away from her own.

Fay shook her head numbly, mesmerised by the slumbrous fire in his glittering silver eyes.

'You're driving me crazy,' he answered, his voice still soft. He reached up and tangled his long fingers in the softness of her burnished hair, pulling her face even closer to his own, and then his mouth was brushing hers, with aching slowness, torturing and tempting her sweetly until her lips parted beneath his and his kiss deepened, warm and urgent with passion.

Fay's bones seemed to melt beneath the fierce, hungry pressure of his mouth, as it left hers to trail a fiery path over her throat, his tongue exploring the hollows between the small fine bones of her shoulders. She murmured his name achingly, as her fingers clutched at his shoulders, and he lifted his head slowly and gazed into her eyes.

'You're beautiful,' he said thickly. 'And I want you, Fay—I want you now.'

Fay could not resist the hunger in his voice and in his eyes.

'Hold me,' she begged softly, holding out her arms to him, pale promises of delight in the dark still room. She was offering herself to him, wanting him to take what was his already. She was overwhelmed and powerless to fight the feelings he had awakened deep inside her.

But even as she spoke, she saw him shudder, stiffen as he moved from her, putting distance between them as he gained control. He stood before her, tall and powerful, and they stared at each other for long moments, until Fay's arms dropped, humiliation washing over her hotly. She pulled the emerald dress tighter around her throat, feeling inexplicably cheap and almost indecent, before Gabriel's intent silver gaze. He had not spoken and for a second she hated him, feeling repulsion at the sight of him. Shivering uncontrollably and praying with all her might that she would not break down until she got to her bedroom, she scrambled weakly to her feet, her limbs still heavy and languorous. She glanced once more at the man before her, standing still and tense, all traces of passion gone from him, a pulse throbbing heavily at his throat as he stared at her with stormy, narrowed eyes, and then she turned away quickly, moving blindly towards the door.

'Fay—don't go.' His harshly-spoken command stopped her dead in her tracks as she fought an inner battle.

Half of her wanted to run, to get away from him for ever, and the other half, the treacherous, weak half, wanted to stay, wanted to hear his excuses, wanted to be back in his strong brown arms. She wanted to laugh out loud at her foolish idea that they could be friends. She knew now that they would never, ever be friends. Enemies or lovers—this was their choice, and Fay would choose enemies. In the future she would be careful, so careful, not to put herself into a position where he could humiliate her as he had tonight.

With one stride Gabriel was at her side, a strange sad defeat in his eyes as he turned her to face him with gentle hands.

'Don't touch me,' she whispered brokenly, shrugging from his grasp, unable to tear her eyes from his. Even now he could hold her still just by looking at her, and this knowledge angered her.

'How could you?' she accused him bitterly, tears no longer under control trickling down her angry, defiant face. 'I trusted you, and you let me . . . you led me on——'

Gabriel shook his head tiredly. 'No, Fay, I led myself on. You belong to somebody else,' he said flatly.

Fay turned away, stricken, and ran from the room his words echoing in her head. Why, oh, why had she lied to him about her engagement? Her reasons had seemed perfectly feasible and acceptable at the time, but now she felt only regret.

She did not sleep much that night, and it gave her morbid satisfaction to hear Gabriel pacing the floor of the room above her own. He was obviously not sleeping either. Sighing as she tossed and turned in bed, she admitted that she had been lying to herself, accusing him of disgraceful behaviour. His behaviour had been almost honourable. She had tormented him with her hands until he had responded. She had been ready to give herself, would have done had he not drawn back. She had lain in his arms and practically begged him to make love to her. She groaned, pressing her hands against her burning face with shame. Pretending to be promised to someone else, she had forced him to reject her. She would keep well out of his way in future.

Finally she fell asleep, but it was a light, troubled sleep and she woke the next morning feeling dull and listless. She showered and dressed in jeans and a thick blue jumper, by which time she felt a little better. Brushing out her hair vigorously, she tied it carelessly in a ponytail high on the back of her head and then sat in front of the mirror, examining her face carefully for tell-tale signs of her restless night. Her eyes looked a little bruised, but apart from that she looked the same as usual. She would have to eat more, she decided, and try to get some of her lost weight back. Her face was positively thin. Throwing down the hairbrush with a disgruntled sigh, she went downstairs for breakfast.

The lounge was empty, so she went downstairs to the kitchen where she found Sophie and Mrs Bond sorting out the stocks of food in the huge larder.

'Good morning, Fay. How are you this morning?' Sophie paused in her task of counting tins to smile brightly at her niece.

'I'm fine, but I'm afraid I overslept,' Fay replied lightly, determined not to give anything away about the previous night. 'Can I help?'

'No, my dear, but could you make your own breakfast, while we carry on with this?' Sophie asked absently.

'Yes, of course. What's happening?' Fay put two pieces of bread into the toaster.

'We're just making a list of all the provisions we'll need. There's no saying when we'll be able to get into town again, and Gabe's offered to take me in today.'

'I see.' Fay turned away to put the kettle on, blushing furiously at the mention of his name, and cursing herself for doing so. 'Do you think we're going to be snowed in, then?'

'More than likely,' Sophie said dryly. 'It's the same nearly every year. I sometimes wonder why we bother living here at all.'

Fay smiled lovingly at her aunt. 'Because you love this house, you wouldn't leave here for anything.'

Sophie laughed and turned back to her work. Fay buttered her toast and made a pot of tea. She poured two cups for Sophie and Mrs Bond, then sat down to eat her breakfast. She had just finished her toast when Gabriel came into the kitchen silently. Engrossed in her own thoughts, she did not hear him come in, but looked up as she poured herself a cup of tea to find him watching her with grey, unfathomable eyes. Her eyes dropped immediately, embarrassment washing over her.

'What time do you want to leave, Sophie?' she heard him asking.

Sophie appeared from the larder, smiling. 'In about half an hour, if that suits you. Fay's just made some tea, so sit down and have a cup while you're waiting.' She bustled back into the adjoining room, leaving Fay and Gabriel alone in the warm kitchen.

Fay jumped to her feet, nervously, to get another cup and saucer from the dresser. She felt very jumpy in his company, especially after last night, but she could not let him know that, so deciding to appear cool and unmoved by him, she forced herself to sit back down at the table.

'You'll have some tea?' she asked him carefully, her voice a little husky, despite her efforts.

'Yes, please,' he answered politely, pulling out a chair, and sitting down opposite her at the table. She passed him the cup, glancing up as she did so. His hair was damp, curling attractively over his forehead, and he had obviously just taken a shower. He looked lean and fit, if a little tired, in a dark shirt and a jacket superbly tailored to his broad shoulders.

'Have you had breakfast?' She smiled at him warily as she asked.

'And if I haven't, will you make some for me?' he questioned lazily, a smile playing at the corners of his mouth.

'Yes, I suppose so.'

He stared at her for a moment. 'You look like a child with your hair that way,' he said softly, his eyes on the long sweep of her exposed neck, as he lit a cigarette.

Fay snorted. 'Well, if you're going to be rude. . . .' she began angrily.

'You also look as if you didn't sleep too well last night. Am I right?' he asked, openly amused at her anger.

'That's none of your business!' she flashed, wishing that she had gone when her inner self had urged her to. The conversation was getting far too personal.

'It might have been,' Gabriel said softly, shamelessly reminding her of the passion that had flared between them, his voice a caress. Fay took a long shaky breath.

'Do you want any breakfast or not?' she repeated coldly, biting back the angry and accusing words, she wanted to hurl at him.

'I'm not hungry, thank you,' he replied flatly, and Fay knew that he was angry. He stubbed out his cigarette with vicious fingers, his mouth tight and uncompromising. Why couldn't they get on? Fay thought wearily.

'We'll never be friends, you know that,' Gabriel stated harshly, reading her mind.

She looked up at him, her eyes wide and startled, green and pure in the bright morning light of the kitchen.

'Yes, I know that now,' she admitted finally. 'But I think we ought to make some sort of an effort for Sophie.' She did not mean to sound so grudging, but she knew that it came out that way.

'I agree,' Gabriel replied, his voice almost brutal, his eyes like ice as they flicked coldly over her. 'Every effort must be made in front of Sophie.'

'Gabriel, please. . . .' she began, but he cut across her.

'Tell me, Fay, why don't you wear a ring? Don't you think you owe it to your fiancé, or doesn't he mind you acting like a free woman?' he asked cruelly, his face twisted. Fay knew that he was thinking of the night before, and his cutting remarks rekindled her shame and embarrassment and with these feelings, her anger. How dared he speak to her like this? she fumed. She longed to show him that he meant nothing to her, that he could not hurt her, humiliate her or affect her in any way.

She glared at him, her face suffused with colour, her emerald eyes like fire.

'You have no right to judge—you know nothing about the situation between Sam and myself,' she snapped. That at least was true, she added silently to herself, feeling hysterical, her anger dying as quickly as it had burst into life. This argument was so futile, it was almost funny.

Gabriel was staring at her with angry eyes, as a smile she could not control curved her soft mouth.

'Something amuses you?' he asked grimly, looking as if he would like to strangle her with his bare hands.

Fay laughed out loud. 'Yes, you,' she replied with glinting eyes. 'You're so damned self-righteous! Don't forget your life is public property, and while you accuse me of playing around do you think I don't know about you? Your affairs with married women? My God, you make me laugh!' She peered at him with huge, innocent eyes, moistening her lips with the tip of her tongue, unaware of how provocative she seemed. 'Besides, why should it matter to you? Perhaps I want some experience before I marry. No doubt you would condemn me for doing what you do yourself,' she said softly.

Gabriel swore angrily, viciously, getting to his feet with one graceful movement and striding towards the window, where he stood with his back to her, his hands clenched into fists at his side.

'Is that what last night was all about? Experience?'

he asked harshly, turning to face her suddenly, his face a taut mask of unyielding anger.

Fay knew that she had won. She had found the perfect way to hit back at him for rejecting her so cruelly, for treating her feelings so carelessly. His pride.

'Yes,' she said clearly, a small cruel smile playing around her mouth.

Gabriel's breath was drawn in on a hiss. 'You bitch,' he muttered tautly. 'You'll regret this, Fay. You want experience? Come here and I'll give you experience, lady.' His voice was soft now, soft and seductive.

Fay felt the treacherous shudder of response from deep inside herself to the soft, intense timbre of his voice. She stood up, ignoring him, and gathered the dishes together from the table, carrying them to the sink with shaking hands, to begin washing them. She did not look at him, but she felt his eyes boring into her back as she worked.

'What's the matter, scared?' he taunted softly.

Fay swallowed convulsively, wondering if her one hollow moment of victory had been worth all this. But at that moment Sophie appeared, and she was saved. Her aunt was smiling brightly, seemingly unaware of the tense, strained atmosphere in the kitchen.

'I'm nearly ready, Gabe, sorry to keep you waiting so long. Will you be coming with us, Fay?'

Fay paled visibly. 'Not unless you need some help. I thought I'd go for a walk,' she replied, carefully adding a touch of false lightness to her voice.

'No, we won't need any help, so you don't need to come. By the way, did Gabe tell you about dinner tonight?'

Sophie was busy checking things off on the enormous list in her hand, her voice vague. Fay glanced at Gabriel curiously. His anger was well under control now and he was remote, cool and unreadable, only the faint tension in his body giving him away. He did not speak, merely stared at her with cold eyes. Fay turned back to Sophie awkwardly.

'Er ... no. Is somebody coming?' she asked brightly.

'Tell her, Gabe,' Sophie smiled vaguely at him, her attention still with her shopping.

Gabriel's mouth twisted mockingly as he looked at Fay.

'I'd like to take you and Sophie out to dinner tonight. It may be our last chance if we're to be snowed in.' His voice was expressionless, his eyes cool beneath their heavy lids. He gave the impression that he did not give a damn whether Fay went or not, and she curled up inside, regretting what she had said to him. She could not bear to spend the evening with him, she would have to get out of it somehow.

'It's very kind of you, but I . . .' she began, desperately trying to think of a feasible, acceptable excuse.

'Yes, it is kind,' Sophie cut in, with shining eyes. 'I'm so looking forward to it. It seems ages since I went out to dinner.'

Fay watched the excitement and enthusiasm lighting her aunt's face with a sinking heart. She could not refuse Gabriel's invitation, she had no excuse, and she could not spoil it for Sophie. She lifted her head to find him watching her with sardonic interest. She managed a weak smile.

'Yes—it's a lovely idea. Thank you,' she murmured quietly, holding on to her dignity grimly, inexplicably hurt by the savage twist of his lips at her words.

'It's my pleasure,' he returned urbanely, the rough triumph in his eyes clearly visible.

The dishes finished, Fay had every excuse to escape from the kitchen, which was rapidly becoming terribly claustrophobic.

'Have a good day in town, Sophie,' she murmured as she made her way to the door.

'Thank you, dear. Shall I bring anything back for you?'

'No, I don't think so. I'll see you later.'

Fay slipped out of the room quickly, breathing a huge sigh of pure relief. It was almost like being released from a cage, the freedom she felt, just to be away from Gabriel Winter. She rushed upstairs to her room and sat down on the old wicker chair in front of the fire. She felt suddenly young and alive. At least he had done that for her, brought her back to life, after the misty half-world she had been existing in since her illness.

She wondered why she had lied to him so often, letting him think she was a cheat, encouraging him in these thoughts. She was out of her depth with him, afraid of any kind of relationship with him. A question hit her with startling impact. Did she love him? It was impossible and ridiculous, and she got tremblingly to her feet, shocked by her own thoughts. She would go for a walk—anything to take her mind off self-revelation.

Running downstairs, she pulled on her coat and boots and left the house, strolling slowly down the drive. She had noticed the Land Rover parked in front of the house and now she saw Gabriel clearing the snow from the path with a shovel. She watched every movement of his body as she walked up to him, and as if sensing her presence, he straightened and watched her approach with inscrutable eyes.

'Where are you going?' he asked, as she came level with him.

'For a walk,' Fay answered shortly, not meeting his eyes, her glance firmly fixed on his black boots. Something in his tone rankled her.

'Well, don't go too far,' he ordered coldly.

'Why don't you mind your own damned business?' she snapped back at him, hating him for the deep feelings he aroused in her.

'You are my business, now,' he said grimly, something in his voice significant and vaguely threatening.

Fay shivered. 'I'll go as far as I like,' she retorted childishly, 'and you can't stop me.'

Gabriel shrugged, a cruel smile playing at the corners of his hard mouth.

'Don't bet on it, Fay,' he muttered dangerously, reaching out to touch her fiery hair with cruel fingers.

She shied away from him like a frightened horse, her emerald eyes clouded with fear, and strode away, trying not to hear his soft chuckle as he began work again.

She walked out of the gates, across the road and into the white fields beyond. There was a great pleasure in trudging through the snow, and she tried to push thoughts of Gabriel to the back of her mind, determined to enjoy her day. Walking to the top of the hill, she stopped to look down at the house. It sat serenely in the pale sunlight, wedged between two gently sloping hills. A beautiful house, thought Fay, as she stared down at it, huge and grand, a remnant of a past age. Made of Yorkshire stone, its rows of mullioned windows glinted in the sunlight like winking eyes, a huge square building with a high pointed roof and a stone porch, various outbuildings scattered around the back of it. It was very isolated, small wonder that they were often cut off in winter, thought Fay. She really would have to try and persuade her aunt to have a telephone installed, especially now that she was getting older. There was no saying how long Gabriel would stay, next year Sophie could be alone, and Fay knew from experience that when the house became cut off,

Mrs Bond did not come in. Yes, she would have a talk with Sophie that evening.

Sticking her hands deep into her pockets, still pondering on this problem, she trudged over the top of the hill and continued her walk.

She had been walking for over an hour when she heard strange, eerie cries coming from the direction of a hedgerow, almost completely covered with snow. The hedge was below her, running the length of a deep gully to one side of the field she was in. Fay made her way towards the gully, the haunting cries still ringing in her ears, making her feel vaguely frightened, and suddenly very alone.

Chiding herself sternly for letting her imagination run away with her, she reached the edge of the gully and began picking her way carefully down the steep incline. She could see nothing, but the noise was unmistakable—an animal in pain. But suddenly her foot struck something hard, jagged and uneven beneath the thick blanket of snow, and she lost her balance.

She clutched wildly at thin air, hoping to steady herself, but there was nothing to hold on to and with a fierce stab of pain in her ankle she fell to the ground, her leg twisting painfully and awkwardly beneath her, as she hit the snow. Sick with pain for some minutes, she tried to gather her wits, manoeuvring her leg from beneath her body, wincing with the pain that the movement gave her. She explored her leg with her fingers, trying to pinpoint her injury. It seemed to be her ankle and she prayed that it was not broken. The next thing to do was to try to get back on her feet. She took a few deep breaths, inwardly calming herself, waiting a few moments before she tried. It cost her a great deal of effort and pain, but she finally stood up, to find that she could not put any weight at all on her injured ankle. The slightest pressure on it made her dizzy with agony and although she fought it tears of pain and worry began rolling down her cheeks. How would she get back to the house? She had no idea of the time, but it would be dark sooner or later. Panic gripped her at the thought of a night spent out there alone.

Nobody knew where she had gone. The animal was still howling and Fay wanted to scream, it was all too much to bear. So she gave herself up to the luxury of her tears and sobbed noisily.

Finally she quietened, feeling a good deal better and grimly resigned to her predicament. The light seemed to be fading and she looked around for somewhere, anywhere to shelter. There was a loose stone wall at the corner of the field and she hobbled towards it, crying with pain and falling over a good many times. At last she reached it, and scraping the snow off the top she levered herself into a sitting position.

Thankful for her thick, waterproof fur coat, she stuck her hands in her pockets, laughing out loud as her gloved fingers encountered an old, nearly empty packet of cigarettes, and her lighter. Luxury indeed! They must have been there for months, she thought delightedly, as she lit one and drew the smoke in deeply, feeling almost happy. At least it was not snowing and she felt no ill-effects at all, apart from the painful throbbing in her ankle. But however brave she felt, she did not want to think about the approaching night. She was very hungry, and feeling colder by the minute. Please let someone find me, she prayed.

CHAPTER FOUR

As if in a dream, Fay heard her name being called and sat bolt upright on the wall. Had she been asleep? She looked round hopefully. It was still not dark, in fact it was difficult to tell what time of day it was. She heard the call again and with a rush of happiness knew it was Gabriel. She called his name joyfully and then he appeared over the rise of the hill, making his way towards her. Her heart was hammering as he arrived in front of her. She was so glad to see him, his strong lean face, so familiar, so dear to her. She would not have to spend a cold and lonely night out here after all, and she was filled with gratitude and love.

She smiled at him, her heart in her eyes, but he was angry, very angry.

'What the hell do you think you're playing at?' he asked savagely, his eyes black with anger, his mouth thin and frightening.

The smile faded from Fay's lips, and she swallowed nervously, bruised by his anger, tears filling her eyes.

'Please don't be angry with me,' she pleaded softly. 'I thought I'd have to stay here all night. I'm so glad to see you. Please, Gabriel. . . .'

He swore angrily under his breath.

'God, Fay, I warned you! Are you hurt?'

Fay began crying in earnest, sobs shaking her slender body, unable to answer him. Raw and vulnerable, she felt unable to bear his anger, his cruelty.

Gabriel ran his hand through his hair, staring at her for a moment, then he groaned heavily and reaching

out, touched her face gently, wiping away her tears
with strong, brown fingers.

'I'm sorry for making you cry, my love. I didn't
mean to hurt you,' he said quietly, his gentleness
soothing her, making her whole again. 'I was out of
my mind with worry, and I overreacted. Forgive me.'

Fay forced a weak, wet smile. 'It doesn't matter. I
... I've hurt my ankle—I can't walk on it,' she
admitted, feeling foolish.

Gabriel shrugged. 'I'll carry you,' he replied.

'All that way?' She stared at him incredulously.

He smiled at her. 'Why not? I'll enjoy it,' he said
wickedly, and Fay flushed hotly.

Then she remembered the animal. It was silent now
and she hoped it was not dead. She tugged at his sleeve
like a worried child.

'Gabriel, there's an animal in that hedge, I think it's
trapped. It was howling before, and that's why I came
down here. Will you go and see?'

Her eyes pleaded with him and he nodded immediately and walked over to the hedge. She watched
him as he went, tall and strong—she felt safe with him,
she loved him.

He was cursing violently and as she looked, she saw
the object of his anger. He had pushed back a small
part of the hedge, and beneath was a young fox, caught
by its leg in a rusty trap. Gabriel's face was grim as
he forced open the jaws of the trap and released the
fox's leg.

The young animal became quiet and still, and Fay
watched as he examined its injured leg with gentle fingers. He pulled a small silver flask from his coat pocket
and splashed some liquid on to the injured leg before
shooing the animal away, watching as it limped off.

He picked up the trap and walked back to Fay, his
face still grim. It was an old trap, vicious and lethal,

and he smashed it almost symbolically against the stone wall until it broke.

'That trap, at least, won't kill or maim any more animals,' Gabriel said bitterly, and Fay smiled at him, her heart unguarded for a moment, loving him because he cared.

'Will the fox be all right?' she asked worriedly.

Gabriel frowned. 'I think so. The leg wasn't broken. It can't have been trapped long—it was injured fairly badly, though. I put some brandy on it, that should stop any infection spreading.'

Fay sighed. 'It's so cruel. Foxes are so beautiful, and wild and free. How can people trap them?'

'Farmers consider them vermin—nothing is cruel for vermin. But I agree with you, dear soft-hearted Fay, they are beautiful, and freedom is their right,' he said.

Fay stared at him, feeling a glow of warmth around her heart. He was so gentle, so caring of life, so angry at unnecessary cruelty. She was discovering things about him and she wanted to know more, everything. He passed her the flask.

'Drink,' he commanded. 'It will keep you warm until we get back.'

Fay took the flask and swallowed a mouthful, coughing and choking as it flowed like fire down her throat.

'Are you cold?' Gabriel asked her, as he stowed the flask away in the pocket of his coat.

'No,' she answered emphatically.

'Let's go, then, shall we?'

She nodded, and helping her down off the wall, he swung her into his arms, effortlessly, as if she was a child. She felt the powerful muscles of his arms, tight and hard, beneath and around her and slid her own arms around his neck.

'How did you find me so quickly?' she asked, staring at his mouth, fascinating in such close proximity.

'I saw which way you went this morning and followed your tracks,' he explained,.

As he talked, Fay could see his teeth, strong and white and even, one of them flashing gold, and for some reason the sight of them made her heart beat faster.

'Is Sophie worried?' she asked, just for something to say, something to take her mind off the man in whose arms she rested.

'Sophie's not back from town,' Gabriel replied. 'We finished the shopping, then she met an old friend, who'll drive her back this afternoon. The last I saw of them, they were walking along to the tea-shop chatting away nineteen to the dozen!' he finished dryly, and Fay laughed, the picture he painted so vivid in her mind.

Gabriel was walking quickly, holding her easily, and she was amazed at his strength.

'You're very strong.' The words were out before she realised that she had spoken and she cringed inwardly, hot colour flooding her cheeks. What a stupid thing to say!

Gabriel laughed. 'You're very light,' he answered wryly, putting her at ease. Unable to stop herself, Fay examined his face. His eyelashes were long, unusual in a man, and close to she saw that his eyes were flecked with black, making the grey of his pupils seem darker at a distance. She also noticed for the first time that he had a faint scar on his left cheek, a thin uneven white line from his cheekbone to his jaw. It would be invisible in certain light, and she was still wondering at its cause when he caught her looking at it and read the expression in her eyes.

'Nothing romantic, I'm afraid,' he teased. 'A fight—a broken bottle.'

Fay shivered, imagining him, cut and bleeding. 'You fight?' she asked provocatively.

'Only when I have to,' Gabriel replied shortly. 'This

was a long time ago. Alex and I had a misspent youth.'

At that moment the house came into view below them and Fay stared at him in amazement.

'A short cut,' he said amusedly.

Twenty minutes later they were inside. Gabriel put her down long enough to pull her coat from her shoulders, then lifted her up again and carried her to a chair by the fire in the lounge. He lifted her foot on to a small embroidered footstool and ordered her to sit still until he got back.

Fay sank comfortably into the chair with no intention of moving. It was far too warm and bright, all the more so since her narrow escape from spending the night in a cold snowy field. There was no sign of Sophie, and Fay smiled, imagining her still chatting to her friend. She did not want to think of Gabriel now; she would wait until she was alone in her room and then she would re-live the time she had spent in his arms, committing to memory everything that had happened.

He came back into the lounge then carrying a bowl of water and some bandages.

'Do you want a drink?' he asked, smiling at her.

'No, thank you. A cup of tea would be lovely, though,' she said, flashing him a helpless look.

'I'll make one in a moment,' he grinned, and knelt at her feet, unzipping her boots and pulling them off.

Fay gasped with pain, biting her lip to stop herself crying out, when he removed the boot on her injured foot. He gently pulled off the brightly coloured woollen socks that she wore beneath her boots and rolled up the leg of her jeans, his hands cool against the bare skin of her leg. Then he explored the fine bones of her ankle with strong soothing fingers, watching her face carefully for signs of pain.

'It's not broken,' he reassured her gently, 'just badly sprained, I think.'

He bathed her ankle with ice-cold water from the bowl, then bandaged it firmly after applying a cold compress.

'Thank you,' Fay stammered, still feeling embarrassed. 'And thank you for coming to find me, and bringing me back here.' She leaned forward and kissed his cheek, feeling him stiffen even as she did so, cursing herself for her impulsive action.

'It was nothing,' Gabriel replied brusquely, getting to his feet with one agile movement, a muscle twitching in his jaw. 'I'll make some tea.'

He left the room and Fay leaned back in her chair, closing her eyes, as misery engulfed her. They were never at ease with each other, and she felt hurt.

He returned some minutes later balancing a tray of tea in one hand. With her eyes still closed, Fay did not hear him until he touched her shoulder.

'Fay, are you all right?'

Her eyes snapped open and she stared up into his face. He was standing over her, concern mirrored in his grey eyes.

'Yes—I'm fine,' she replied lightly, not feeling fine at all. The whole day had been one long disaster. The only good thing was the fact that she had the perfect excuse for skipping dinner with Sophie and Gabriel that evening.

She watched Gabriel's hands as he poured out two cups of tea. Strong, lean brown hands, hands that could hold and soothe, hands that could give ecstasy.

'Sugar?'

His low voice brought her back to her senses.

'No—thank you,' she answered lamely, not knowing what to say to him.

The silence stretched between them like a barrier, shutting them off from each other, leaving them alone. Gabriel handed her a cup, then sat back and lit a cigarette, his shoulders hunched and tense, his face unreadable. Fay drank her tea quietly, peering at him every now and then over the rim of her cup.

'How long will it be before I can walk on my foot?' she asked at last, unable to bear the silence that was stretching her nerves like wire.

Gabriel shrugged, his eyes distant. 'Two or three days, I imagine. Maybe you should see a doctor.'

Fay flinched at his casual reply.

'No, no, I don't want to see a doctor. They frighten me, somehow. Besides, I saw enough doctors when I was ill. . . .' She stopped abruptly, aware that he was not listening.

'Fay, why did you kiss me just now?' His voice was tense, carefully controlled as he waited for her answer.

Fay flushed, wishing he had not asked. She wondered what his reaction would be if she told him the truth—Because I think I love you.

Gabriel was still watching her, unknown emotion flickering in his clear eyes, at the conflict on her lovely face.

'Because . . . because I wanted to thank you for . . . for everything you'd done. . . . It was an impulse. Oh, why must you embarrass me so?' she cried, turning her face from him, her hands moving nervously in her lap.

In a moment he was at her side, tilting her face towards him with gentle fingers.

'Forgive me, that was very clumsy,' he muttered sincerely, his voice strained. 'I thought we could set things straight between us.'

Fay allowed her eyes to meet his, the impact sending violent shocks through her entire body. They looked deep into each other's eyes, and time seemed to stand still. She could see her own reflection in the clouded grey of Gabriel's eyes and it was as if they had become one person. She was suprememly aware of every slight movement he made, every breath he took seemed to come from her lungs, every beat of his heart belonged to her. Self-betrayal became unimportant as he slowly lowered his head and there seemed to be no passion between them, only a need that went as deep as their souls and injured them both, when his mouth touched hers. His arms came around her and they clung together tightly, until the slam of the front door shutting drove them both apart.

Sophie appeared in the doorway, smiling as ever, removing her coat.

'Is there any tea left in that pot?' she asked brightly, taking in the scene before her—Gabriel standing tall and tense, Fay looking pale and shaken, her green eyes almost feverish.

Moving into the room, Sophie caught sight of the bandage on her niece's ankle and her face crumpled with concern.

'Fay, my dear, what's happened?'

Fay smiled reassuringly. 'I've sprained my ankle, that's all—there's nothing to worry about, honestly!'

'But how, where?' Sophie sat down, hardly noticing the cup of tea that Gabriel pressed into her hands.

'I went for a walk this morning, as you know. I heard an animal howling and when I went to find it, I tripped on something, and that's how it happened. Gabriel found me and brought me back. It doesn't even hurt very much now,' Fay finished encouragingly.

'But how will you manage?' Sophie frowned, imagining all the difficulties involved.

'I'll carry her, whenever necessary,' Gabriel answered firmly. 'She should be able to walk on it in a couple of days.'

Sophie nodded. 'Fay, shouldn't you see the doctor? Gabe would go for him, wouldn't you?'

Gabriel nodded. 'Of course.'

'I don't want to see a doctor,' Fay cut in firmly. 'It's only a sprain, please don't worry, Sophie.'

'I can't help it—you seem so fragile, and all this so soon after your illness.'

'Sophie!' Fay exclaimed with exasperation. 'The only thing this sprained ankle will stop me from doing is going out to dinner tonight. But you two must go, I insist—and I'll be perfectly all right,' she finished sternly, seeing Sophie opening her mouth to protest.

Sophie, however, was not to be put off. 'Oh, Fay, you must come!' she insisted. 'Gabriel can carry you to the car, and to the restaurant. I wouldn't dream of leaving you alone in the house.'

Fay glanced at Gabriel, who had been silent throughout. He was watching her with cool unfathomable eyes. Sighing, she realised that there was no reason why she should not go out, not the way Sophie told it. 'Very well, I'll come,' she agreed. 'But I'd like to go to my room now.'

Gabriel got to his feet, his eyes glinting, his mouth amused. He picked her up gently and Fay closed her eyes wearily. She was fighting a losing battle—Gabriel, Sophie—she did not have a chance.

'I'll pop in and see you later,' her aunt promised as they left the room.

Gabriel carried her effortlessly upstairs. 'The perfect excuse?' he murmured cryptically, obviously still amused.

Fay ignored him, keeping her eyes closed and fighting the urge to punch him on the nose. He laid her on her bed.

'Thank you,' she whispered, opening her eyes at last. 'What time is it?'

'Nearly five.'

'What time are we leaving?' she asked defeatedly.

Gabriel misunderstood her tired defeat for apathy

and irritation tightened his firm mouth.

'Goddammit, Fay, I won't force you to come!' he muttered furiously, and turning on his heel, quickly strode from the room, leaving his anger almost tangible around her like a shroud. She shivered, even though the room was warm from the bright fire burning in the small hearth.

Relaxing on the bed, she went over the day's events in her mind. She could not believe that it was only five o'clock, the day seemed to have lasted for ever. She must have fallen asleep, because she woke up to find the room in darkness, and Sophie knocking on her door.

'It's nearly seven, Fay, and we'll be leaving at eight.' She switched on the light and walked over to draw the curtains.

Fay struggled into a sitting position blinking in the light.

'Do you want any help getting ready?' Sophie asked briskly.

'No, I can manage, I think, but thanks for the offer.'

'I'll leave you to it, then, I have to get changed myself. Isn't it lovely, going out to dinner?' Sophie bustled from the room, her face wreathed in smiles, and Fay smiled too. She would not spoil Sophie's evening—and yes, it would be nice to go out for dinner. She struggled to her feet, placing most of her weight on her uninjured foot, then gingerly tried to walk. It was difficult and very painful, but she managed to hobble to the bathroom to wash.

That done, back in her bedroom, she sank on to the ornate stool in front of the dressing-table with relief and began her make-up. She applied a light foundation and powder, then turned her attention to her eyes. She stroked glistening green shadow on to her eyelids and darkened her lashes with mascara. The effect was stunning; her eyes glowed like precious stones, huge and mysterious in her small face. She applied lipstick carefully, then brushed her hair until it shone.

She had already decided on a dress. It was full-length, which would hide the bandage on her swollen ankle, a beautiful velvet gown in green and russet brown, the colours blending and swirling together to give a misty effect. The style was simple, round-necked and long-sleeved, and it hugged the curved shape of her body lovingly, flaring out below her hips to float around her small feet.

She slipped into the dress and studied the completed picture carefully in the mirror. She looked almost beautiful, she thought happily; the colours of the dress accentuated her glowing eyes and burnished hair. She slipped her feet into flat green velvet evening slippers—high heels were out of the question—and as a finishing touch, put silver loops through her ears. She was ready.

Limping over to the bed, she sat down to wait for Gabriel to take her downstairs. She would be polite but cool, she decided, the trouble being that things tended to get out of hand whenever they were together. A knock on the door heralded his punctual arrival.

'Come in,' she called, unprepared for the shock of his appearance as he stood before her. He took her breath away, totally male and devastatingly attractive, in a pale grey shirt and tie and a black dinner jacket, superbly tailored to his broad shoulders. Matching black trousers moulded his long legs, and the whole effect was magnificent. A supremely confident male animal, exuding a magnetism that left Fay weak and trembling.

He smiled at her, his clear eyes appraising her very thoroughly from beneath heavy lids.

'You're ready,' he stated huskily. Fay nodded

dumbly. She could see how beautiful she was in his slumbrous eyes, in the sensual twist of his mouth. There was no need for words, and her heart began to hammer wildly.

He slid his hands beneath her and lifted her against his broad chest. His face was so near her own and she wanted to touch him, to explore with her fingers and her lips the hard bones and hollows of his strong face. Instead, she rested her head lightly against his shoulder, breathing in the clean male scent of him, mingled with the faint tang of after-shave.

Sophie was waiting for them downstairs, looking splendid in a pale blue dress, her usually wild, greying hair brushed into a neat and stylish chignon.

'Sophie, you look lovely!' Fay exclaimed as Gabriel put her down.

'Thank you, my dear,' Sophie beamed, touched by Fay's sincere praise. 'You look quite breathtaking, doesn't she, Gabe?'

'Beautiful,' Gabriel murmured, his voice rough and strange as he turned away to see to the car.

Fay watched him go with sad eyes, her heart suddenly heavy.

Then they were in the car, and on their way. Fay insisted on sitting in the back, leaving Sophie in the front with Gabriel. Her excuse that she wanted to be able to stretch out and rest her foot was met with a mocking twist of Gabriel's lips. She sat silently, wrapped in her thick emerald green velvet cloak, warm and content just to listen to Sophie chatting to Gabriel in the front. He was attentive and polite, but Fay sensed that his attention was elsewhere. She looked up to find him staring at her through the rear-view mirror with veiled, intent eyes. She lowered her head quickly, feeling again the shock of raw emotion that any contact with him brought in its wake. She kept her head down for the rest of the journey, aware of his eyes on her from time to time.

At last they reached the restaurant, warmth, light and noise issuing from its exclusive doors.

'If you help me, I think I can walk,' she said to Gabriel as he swung open the car door for her.

'You shouldn't try to walk,' he replied crisply.

'Please, Gabriel, it would be so embarrassing to be carried in,' she pleaded.

'Very well,' he answered, his eyes softening as he stared into her upturned face.

He helped her out of the car and into the restaurant, supporting her discreetly but strongly. They were shown to their table by a hovering respectful waiter and Fay glanced around with interest.

A small band played quietly at one end of the room and there was a tiny dance floor in front. The clientele oozed wealth and respectability. They had just ordered their meal and were sipping pre-dinner drinks when Sophie pointed out two people just entering the restaurant.

'Gabe, isn't that Lucy and John Baxter over there by the door?' Gabriel turned his head and Fay did too, her eyes on Lucy Baxter, remembering what Sophie had said about her. She was a stunning young woman, small and blonde, her perfect figure shimmering in white, and Fay took an instant irrational dislike to her, suddenly feeling drab and dowdy by comparison.

Lucy had spotted Gabriel and was making her way towards their table, a sweet smile on her face, as she dragged her father behind her. Close to, Fay could see that she was quite beautiful. But her pale blue eyes were hostile and cold as they rested on Fay and Sophie for a second before she turned her full charming attention on Gabriel, who was smiling indulgently at her. A jealous chill settled round Fay's heart as Lucy insisted, and Gabriel agreed, that the Baxters join them. She examined Lucy Baxter closely while they waited for extra chairs. The other girl's shining blonde hair was coiled into an elaborate knot on the top of her head, leaving her delicate chin and long white neck open to inspection. Her face was expertly made up, and her white dress flattered her curved figure. She was lovely, but Fay could clearly see the coldness in her, and wondered spitefully what Gabriel saw in her.

Her father John, however, seemed pleasant and open. He too had fair hair and a strong open honest face. It was obvious that there was strong affection and deep friendship between him and Gabriel.

Introductions were made and Lucy squeezed herself between Gabriel and John, to both Fay and Sophie's disgust. However, at that moment the food arrived, diverting further comment. Fay ate her pâté with relish, suddenly hungry, realising that she had eaten nothing since breakfast. Glancing up, she found Lucy's malicious eyes on her and smiled blandly. Gabriel was charming and witty, easing the tension around the table, and despite herself Fay was captivated. He was devastating, his charm completely natural, and it was an effort to drag her eyes away from him. Lucy Baxter was obviously having the same trouble.

Later, Lucy asked Gabriel to dance, pouting prettily at him. Fay giggled, unable to stop herself, at Sophie's disgusted snort, and they were both rewarded with a hostile stare. Fay knew what Sophie was thinking and loved her for it. She watched Lucy and Gabriel dancing, her eyes riveted, hardly paying any attention to John who was entertaining both Sophie and herself charmingly. Lucy was flirting unashamedly with Gabriel, her arms wound around his neck as they danced. He was smiling at her and Fay turned away, sick with jealousy. She wanted to go home, she felt as if she had been in the restaurant for hours, as she tried to disguise her quiet desperation. Gabriel and Lucy returned to the table, Lucy hanging possessively on his arm, and Fay found his eyes on her. She saw his concern and smiled at him. She would not let him see her jealousy.

At last, it was time to leave. Fay could feel Lucy's eyes upon them as Gabriel helped her from the restaurant. Once in the car she settled back and closed her eyes, comfortably replete and rather tired. Glancing at the clock on the dashboard she saw that it was after midnight. Her ankle was throbbing painfully, and she longed to be in bed. She dozed on and off until they reached the house, and Gabriel, ignoring her protests, taking heed only of the pain in her eyes as she tried to walk, swung her into his arms and carried her upstairs to her room. He deposited her gently on the bed, then sat down beside her, loosening his tie with a weary gesture.

'You didn't enjoy yourself tonight,' he stated flatly, pinning her down with his merciless eyes.

'Yes, I did,' Fay protested. 'If I was quiet, it was because my ankle was hurting,' she lied.

'Why do you lie to me, Fay?' he asked quietly.

'I think you'd better leave,' she said, ignoring his question and turning away from him.

'I'm not leaving until you answer my question,' he replied, his voice soft and dangerous.

'I don't lie to you,' Fay said loudly.

'Tell me, what do you think of Lucy Baxter?' he asked, changing the subject unexpectedly and grasping her shoulders, as he turned her to face him.

'She's very beautiful and I'm sure she's a very nice girl,' Fay answered evasively, her weak words of praise giving her away.

'Liar!' His softly spoken answer and knowing smile incensed her.

'Very well, if you want the truth, she's cold and malicious and she'll make you miserable.'

Gabriel smiled, still not releasing her shoulders. 'Why should you care?' he taunted.

'I don't. You wanted the truth and I gave it to you.' Fay answered flatly.

'I suppose that's something,' Gabriel admitted dryly. He leaned over and brushed her lips with his hard mouth. 'Goodnight, Fay.' He got slowly to his feet, looking exhausted.

Fay touched his arm. 'I do thank you for the evening, and I did enjoy it, the meal was lovely,' she said sincerely, wanting to make her peace with him.

Gabriel smiled tiredly. 'I enjoyed it too,' he said softly, his eyes lingering on her face.

'Are all your lady friends as beautiful as Lucy?' Fay asked curiously, not wanting him to go, wanting to hold him.

'Are you my friend, Fay?'

She thought for a moment. 'You said we could never be friends,' she parried, her lips curving into a soft smile.

'There's your answer,' he said cryptically. He touched her cheek gently and left the room, shutting the door quietly behind him.

Fay shook her head, still smiling, and limped over to the window. Outside, from the light of a nearly full moon she could see that it had started snowing again. It was beautiful, and she stood transfixed for many moments, her thoughts sad. Was there something serious between Gabriel and Lucy Baxter? Sophie didn't think so, and that was some consolation, but it did little to ease the worry and jealousy inside her. Lucy would not make him happy, he needed someone warm and gentle. You? she asked herself mockingly, and sighed heavily. Yes, me. I love him.

She looked down and saw him coming out of the house. He lifted his face to the snow as she watched in a strange, defeated gesture. Then he flung away the cigarette he had been smoking and got into the car, driving it slowly round to the back of the house and out of view. Fay wondered why he did not get enough sleep—so many questions, and she had no answers.

She limped to the bathroom to wash, meeting Sophie on the landing.

'How's the ankle?' asked her aunt.

'Aching!' Fay replied ruefully. 'It was a lovely meal, though, wasn't it?'

Sophie snorted. 'It was until Lucy Baxter got there.'

Fay smiled sadly. 'Oh, Sophie, what can you do if Gabriel loves her?'

'He doesn't love her,' Sophie retorted.

'You were so funny in the restaurant,' Fay giggled, 'snorting every time Lucy opened her mouth!'

Sophie smiled reluctantly, feeling ashamed. 'I couldn't help it,' she admitted. 'She's such a dreadful girl. When she asked Gabriel if you were disabled, I nearly smacked her face!'

'I didn't hear that—what did he say?' Fay stared at her aunt curiously, a smile on her face.

'I didn't catch his answer, but whatever it was it shut her up good and proper! He was annoyed with her,' Sophie said wisely. 'She glared at everybody for at least five minutes.'

They both laughed.

'She's not a very tactful girl, obviously,' Fay remarked, puzzled by Gabriel's reaction to Lucy's question.

'She's wild, that one. I expect it's because she's never had a mother,' Sophie continued, seeing Fay's look of interest. 'Her mother walked out on John, leaving Lucy with him, just after she was born.'

'How awful, for both of them!' Fay exclaimed, feeling compassion for both John and Lucy. That explained a lot of Lucy's behaviour and, she thought hopefully, Gabriel's kindness to her. She walked towards the bathroom. 'Goodnight, Sophie.' She kissed her aunt and went to wash.

As she lay in bed later, she tried to work things out in her mind, but she was too tired and fell asleep quickly, thinking of Gabriel and hoping for a miracle.

CHAPTER FIVE

LIFE at Lambrigg House went on quietly and uneventfully for a few days. Fay and Sophie did not see much of Gabriel, and assumed that he was either catching up on his sleep or working. He did not come downstairs for meals and Sophie insisted on sending up trays for him. The two women spent their time talking, reading and cleaning. Life was quiet and peaceful, and Fay felt happy. Her ankle was getting better every day, she could walk on it easily now, the only trouble she had from it being a slight aching sometimes at night when she was in bed. She had suffered no other ill-effects from her accident, and she felt well.

But she missed Gabriel, as she had never missed anyone before in her life; she longed to see him. Her opportunity came one night when Sophie asked her if she would take up a tray for him. Fay agreed immediately, a familiar excitement fluttering in her stomach.

She carried the tray upstairs carefully and knocked on his door. There was no answer, so she knocked a little louder, knowing that he was in, because she had heard him typing earlier on.

Balancing the tray carefully in one hand, she opened the door and peeped in. There was no sign of life, but the lights were on.

'Gabriel, it's Fay. I've brought you some dinner!' she called. No answer.

She walked into the small flat, looking round curiously. There was a kitchen, a bathroom and two other

79

rooms; as Sophie had said, it was completely self-contained. She moved into one of the rooms, finding it to be the living room, and set the tray down on a small table. There was no sign of Gabriel, and she could not help looking round—it was so interesting to see where he lived.

There was a huge leather couch near the fire, covered with books and magazines. The walls were a dark Spanish red, scattered with strange, wild abstract paintings. In front of the window stood a huge oak desk, with a typewriter on it, also scattered with papers and books. A comfortable leather chair sat in front of the desk, and one wall was devoted to bookshelves, literally crammed with books. The pale carpet was thick and luxurious, and other items in the room included expensive stereo equipment, a small television and a collection of African carvings. The whole room had a powerfully male atmosphere, and Fay was enchanted with the rich contrasts of colour.

She strolled out of the room intending to find Gabriel. Only one room remained unchecked, and she pushed open the door cautiously. It was the bedroom, and from the soft light of a bedside lamp, she saw Gabriel lying on the bed. He was asleep, the sound of his peaceful breathing filling her ears as she moved automatically towards him. He lay sprawled on the huge bed, dressed only in tight, faded jeans. He had obviously taken a shower before falling asleep, because his hair was still damp and there was a towel beneath his broad, naked shoulders.

Fay stared down at him, desire rising inside her like a tidal wave at the sight of his bare body. Her eyes hungrily explored every inch of his broad chest and the dark hair that matted it, his powerful shoulders and strong, muscular arms. She ached with a longing to touch him. His face, in sleep, was peaceful and untroubled; he looked younger, almost defenceless, and despite herself she reached down and touched his face gently, his cheekbones hard beneath her fingers. She felt dazed by his nearness, his magnificence, breathless and weak.

His eyes snapped open as she touched him, instantly alert, and he reached out for her, pulling her off balance, and down beside him. He rolled on to his side, his muscles rippling beneath his tanned skin, and looked down at her with dark, narrowed eyes.

Fay lay on her back, still dazed and too weak to move, staring back at him with wide, startled eyes.

Gabriel arched over her, holding her captive. He said her name softly, intensely, and her heart began to beat suffocatingly fast.

'Don't you know how dangerous it is to come to a man's room when he's asleep?' he asked huskily, his fingers playing havoc with her senses as they trailed across her throat.

Fay smiled at him innocently. 'No, I've never been in a man's room before. Tell me,' she whispered provocatively, not responsible for her own actions, he overwhelmed her so.

He lowered his head slowly, his eyes smoky and unsmiling as he captured her lips with hungry precision, his kiss deep and shattering, his arms coming around her, pressing her down beneath him on the soft bed. His heavy body was warm, hard and urgent over hers, his mouth was drugging, inducing a response from Fay that she could not control. This was the only place in the world that she wanted to be, and she slid her arms around him, her hands caressing the smooth skin of his back, kissing him, trailing her mouth lovingly over his face.

Gabriel's arms tightened around her, as he fought for control. He felt an almost desperate need to possess her—she was so beautiful, lying in his arms, waiting for his love. But she was young, innocent and untouched, she belonged to another man. He, Gabriel, had no right to her innocence, and he could not take it—God help him.

Fay sensed the withdrawal in him, the tight control over his actions, as he lifted his head to look down at her.

He smiled, dispelling the worry that nagged inside her, and she smiled back. They lay together, wrapped in each other's arms, savouring the peace and comfort they gave to each other.

'Your dinner will be cold,' Fay said at last, her voice still breathless. Gabriel released her immediately and got to his feet, reaching for a shirt and pulling it on, giving her a chance to get up from the bed without embarrassment, which she took.

They walked from the bedroom hand in hand.

'These paintings are beautiful. Did you do them?' Fay asked, gazing at a particularly savage abstract over the fire, with interest and admiration.

Gabriel shook his head. 'No, my brother was the artist.' He glanced up at the painting, his face pained. 'He's dead—killed in a flying accident six months ago.'

Fay stared at him with horror, not knowing what to say. He seemed lost in his own thoughts, as he glanced at her.

'Sophie will be waiting for you,' he said harshly, dismissing her.

Without answering, Fay turned and left the room, and the flat, and went slowly downstairs, a heavy weight around her heart, and an unbearable desire to share his grief. She found Sophie in the dining room.

'What's the matter?' Sophie asked, seeing Fay's stricken face.

'Gabriel has just told me about his brother,' Fay whispered miserably.

Sophie's face sobered. 'It's tragic. He was younger than Gabriel, only thirty when he died.'

'I wish I could help him,' Fay said absently, her mind filled with Gabriel's face, bleak and haunted.

'I don't think he needs help. He must come to terms with it himself,' Sophie replied sadly.

Fay picked at her meal, unaware of Sophie's worried eyes upon her. Her misery had still not gone by bedtime. She lay in bed, listening to Gabriel's movements overhead, longing to go to him but knowing that she couldn't. Sophie was right, he did not need her help. As she fell asleep, she remembered that the following day was her birthday. Sophie would probably forget, she thought, with a secret smile.

Deciding to take Sophie breakfast in bed, Fay got up early the next day. She crept downstairs, to find Gabriel making coffee in the kitchen, whistling softly to himself as he worked.

'Good morning, Fay,' he greeted her with a polite smile. 'Coffee?'

'Yes, please. You're up early,' she said, smiling back at him.

'I have to go out,' he replied briskly, deftly pouring two cups of coffee and handing her one.

'Mrs Bond won't be in today or for quite a while. She's got bronchitis, so I thought I'd take Sophie her breakfast in bed,' Fay told him, repeating what Sophie had told her the previous night. 'Shall I make you some breakfast too?'

'Fattening me up?' Gabriel asked dryly. Fay sighed and he held up his hands in mock horror. 'Okay, okay! I'm sorry. Yes, I'd love some breakfast.'

Fay finished her coffee and got to her feet. 'What

would you like? I'm going to fry bacon and eggs for Sophie.'

'That would be fine. Shall I help?'

'No, I work better alone,' Fay answered quickly, terrified of his nearness.

He watched her every movement as she expertly fried eggs and bacon and made toast. He laid the table while she set out a tray for Sophie, with a pot of tea and some orange juice, all the while nervous under his clear grey scrutiny.

When she finally set his breakfast in front of him he thanked her, his mouth twisting bitterly.

'You're going to make a perfect wife,' he remarked roughly. 'When are you getting married, Fay?'

His tone was brutal and she flinched from it, her green eyes hurt and angry as she turned on him.

'It's none of your business. Leave me alone, Gabriel.'

He ignored her and began eating hungrily, which infuriated her further.

'Did you hear me?' she shouted.

'I could hardly fail to,' he replied nastily, still eating.

Controlling herself with a great effort, Fay picked up Sophie's tray and left the kitchen, kicking the door shut violently behind her. They were constantly at each other's throats. They had moments of perfect passion and moments of bitter enmity—nothing in between. Her relationship with Sam had been so mild and easy-going, with no bitterness between them until the end. She gave up any hope of ever working it out.

Sophie was already awake.

'Oh, Fay, you shouldn't have!' she protested as Fay placed the tray on her lap and went to open the curtains.

'Yes, I should,' Fay replied firmly. 'You deserve it.'

'Did I hear shouting downstairs?' her aunt asked,

sipping her orange juice.

'I'm sorry, did it waken you? It was only Gabriel and me arguing again.' Fay sat down on the edge of her aunt's bed. 'We just can't seem to get on.'

Sophie laughed. 'Well, you know what they say about the path of true love,' she remarked sagely.

'It's hardly that,' Fay protested, blushing.

'Are you sure?'

'I know Gabriel doesn't love me,' Fay said firmly, the words hurting her to say them. 'Anyway, I don't really want to talk about it. Are your eggs how you like them?'

'They're delicious, thank you—and Happy Birthday!'

'You remembered!' Fay laughed, leaning over to kiss her aunt.

'Of course I remembered, and I'm going to bake you a cake this afternoon.'

Fay smiled happily. 'I'll leave you to eat your breakfast in peace, and go and get something for myself.'

She skipped downstairs, happy again. The kitchen was empty, Gabriel's dishes washed and neatly stacked on the draining board. Fay made herself an omelette and some fresh coffee and switched on the radio, glancing round the kitchen fondly as she ate. Such a lovely room, old and warm and shiny. Gabriel had lit the fire, and the bright flames were reflected in the copper pans that hung from the walls and warmed the huge pine table that had been in the kitchen for as long as Fay could remember. It was warm and cosy— the heart of the house. Perhaps she would do some baking today, it was something she enjoyed. She would make a good wife, she told herself grimly, her mellow mood suddenly spoiled.

Gabriel got back about eleven, and strolled into the lounge where Fay was sitting reading, curled up in front of the fire alone. She glanced up at him briefly, then carried on reading, hoping he would go away. But he didn't; instead he held out a huge bunch of daffodils.

'For you,' he said quietly. 'I was cruel to you, I'm sorry.'

Fay got to her feet and took the flowers, burying her face in the sweet-smelling blossoms.

'They're beautiful,' she said huskily, touched by the gesture. 'Thank you. How did you know that daffodils are my favourite flowers?'

He shrugged gracefully. 'I guessed,' he replied laughingly.

'I'll go and put them in water.' She turned to leave the room, but he detained her.

'Wait. I also have these for you.' He pulled several envelopes out of his pocket and handed them to her with a smile.

'Birthday cards!' Fay laughed delightedly, her eyes shining. 'But how . . .?'

'I collected them from the post office while I was there,' he replied casually. 'You ought to have them on your birthday.'

Fay flung her arms around his neck and kissed his mouth. 'Thank you,' she said impulsively. Then, realising what she had done, she withdrew her arms quickly, hot colour staining her cheeks.

'I'm sorry,' she mumbled, not meeting his eyes.

'Forget it,' he muttered harshly, turning towards the window and lighting a cigarette.

Fay picked up her flowers. 'I'll get a vase,' she said, by way of an excuse to leave the room.

She arranged the daffodils carefully in a white china vase, then sat down at the kitchen table to open her birthday cards. There were lots from friends and relations, one from her parents, one from Paul and one from Sam which she left until last. The message was brief, but inside was a note asking if he could come and see her. Fay's heart sank. She did not want to fight with him again, but she would never marry him, her heart belonged to Gabriel. She would not think of it today, she decided; it was her birthday and problems could be put off until tomorrow.

She dressed with special care for dinner that evening. After spending over an hour soaking in a deliciously scented hot bath, she applied her make-up carefully, and brushed out her hair. She chose a cream-coloured silk caftan that she knew suited her perfectly, to wear. It was beautifully cut, and she was aware how fragile it made her look, and she sang softly to herself as she put small emerald earrings, a twenty-first birthday present from her parents, into her ears, and dabbed her pulse spots with her favourite perfume. Then she stood in front of the mirror to consider her appearance. Her eyes were shining and her face was suffused with healthy, becoming colour. She looked stunning. Perhaps Gabriel would fall in love with her tonight.

She ran downstairs, still singing, to help Sophie with dinner. They had made Fay's birthday cake that afternoon from an old recipe, containing honey and almonds. It was covered with chocolate icing, her favourite, and stood in splendour on the kitchen table.

'Do you think I can have a candle on it?' Fay asked, tying on an apron to protect her dress. 'I know it's silly, but it isn't a birthday cake without a candle to blow out, and a wish.'

'I agree,' Sophie replied with a smile, pausing in her task of checking pans of vegetables. 'You'll find some in the cupboard near the door.'

Fay found them and picked out a green one. She stuck it into the middle of the cake and stood back to admire the effect.

'Shall I take it up, and set the table?'

'If you would, my dear.'

'Do you want any help with the cooking?'

'No, it's just a case of waiting now,' Sophie laughed. 'Use the best china, Fay, it is a special occasion, after all.'

'Right!'

Feeling childishly excited, Fay ran upstairs and began setting the table for three. Gabriel had promised to come down for dinner and her heart was full. She put the flowers he had given her in the centre of the table with the birthday cake. She had just finished when Gabriel came in, dark and attractive in a black velvet suit, which accentuated his strong good looks. He smiled at her.

'You look very beautiful,' he murmured slowly, his eyes moving over her.

Fay noticed the bottle in his hand. 'What's that?' she asked, staring at him with hunger glinting in her green eyes.

He handed her the bottle. 'To drink your health.'

'Champagne! How lovely—thank you.' Fay put the bottle on the table and turned back to him. The smile was gone from his eyes.

'Your fiancé won't be coming, I assume?' he asked, looking at the three place settings, his eyes glittering darkly, his voice suddenly angry.

Fay closed her eyes painfully. 'Please, Gabriel, please don't let's fight tonight,' she pleaded with him.

'I'm not fighting,' he replied coldly.

Fay stared at him with tear-filled eyes. 'Damn you,' she whispered clearly.

His mouth tightened, and he strode from the room. Fay took a deep breath, trying to calm herself. Oh, he could be so cruel! Tomorrow she would tell him about Sam, wipe out this lie between them.

She poured herself a gin and tonic and drank it quickly. She was unused to spirits and it made her cough violently, but she could feel its calming effects on her empty stomach immediately.

The meal was an unqualified success—roast beef, roast potatoes and Yorkshire pudding, served with vegetables, cooked to perfection by Sophie, succulent and delicious. Fay drank a lot of wine, trying to ignore the man seated opposite her, whose piercing eyes rested on her so often. Fortunately, he made no mention of the scene between them before dinner, in fact he was as charming and as amusing as ever, which left Fay discomfited.

The wine helped, and by the end of the meal she could look at him, careless defiance lifting her head. She cut the cake after making a wish and they drank her health with Gabriel's champagne. Then Sophie gave Fay her present, wrapped in festive paper.

Fay tore it open with excited fingers, to find beneath the wrapping a richly embroidered shawl, so beautiful that it took her breath away.

'It's exquisite,' she breathed softly. 'Oh, thank you, Sophie!' She kissed her aunt lovingly.

'It belonged to my grandmother, your great-grand-mother. I know you'll love it as much as I have,' her aunt said mistily.

Fay put it around her shoulders. It was soft and scented with lavender—so very beautiful.

Gabriel had been watching her with enigmatic eyes, and now he pulled a small flat package wrapped in silver-coloured paper from his pocket, and held it out to her.

'Happy Birthday, Fay,' he said gently.

Fay took the present from him, feeling quite stunned, opening it with trembling fingers. Under the paper was an old wooden jewel case, polished with care, the wood grain beautifully patterned. She prised open the case and looked inside, shocked into still silence by what she saw. On a bed of rich green velvet lay a necklace of tiny emeralds linked by strands of platinum. The whole thing was breathtaking, created delicately and lovingly by a remarkable craftsman. She looked up at Gabriel to find him watching her, a smile curving his firm mouth, his eyes warm.

She felt near to tears, overcome by his care in choosing this birthday present for her. She turned to Sophie to show her the necklace, but her aunt's seat was empty.

'She's gone to make the coffee,' said Gabriel, his voice low and hypnotic. Fay turned back to him.

'Won't you put it on?' he asked gently.

She felt the silent tears trickling down her face, as she shut the case carefully and handed it back to him.

'I can't keep it,' she whispered.

Gabriel stared at her. 'You don't like it?'

'Of course I like it, it's the most beautiful necklace I've ever seen, but I . . . I can't accept it, you must see that. . . .' Her throat closed up and she could not speak.

Gabriel's head lifted proudly. 'I don't see,' he said coolly. 'Do you think your fiancé would object?'

Fay shook her head dumbly.

'Well then. It's for you and you must accept it, Fay. No other woman could wear it as you will,' he said firmly, opening the case and removing the necklace. It hung from his fingers, ridiculously fragile in his strong hands. 'I'll fasten it for you,' he said softly, brooking no argument. 'Come here.'

Fay wiped away her tears and walked towards him, a small bubble of happiness bursting inside her. She stood in front of him, lifting up her hair, and felt the cold shock of the necklace around her throat, heavy and unknown. Gabriel's cool fingers brushed her skin lightly, making her shiver.

'There.' He turned her round to face him, and she put her hand up to touch the necklace, smiling at him shyly.

'I want to look at it in the mirror.' She walked over to the mirror and studied herself. The necklace lay against her white throat, glittering and beautiful, the exact colour of her tear-washed eyes. Gabriel came up behind her and laid his hands gently on her shoulders, and their eyes met in the mirror. Fay could not move and she was breathing fast as she stared into his eyes, seeing something in them that she almost understood, something just beyond her reach. Why, oh, why couldn't she understand what his eyes were saying to her?

As she watched, he lowered his head and pressed his lips to her neck, causing a violent sensation inside her. He murmured something softly, something that she did not hear, and as she turned to ask him, he swooped, possessing her mouth fiercely, demanding her response as his arms closed around her, strong and hungry.

Fay responded, running her fingers feverishly through the crisp thickness of his dark hair, pressing herself closer to the hard length of his body, reacting to his immediate response. His mouth moved over her face and his hands slid over her slowly, possessively, exploring her slender body with desire he took no care to conceal, and Fay, frightened of the intense response he was arousing in her, pulled away from him suddenly.

Gabriel let her go easily, aware of her unexpected fear, and did not attempt to take her back into his arms. Fay fought to control her treacherous emotions, feeling angry with herself and with him for the way he could make her feel. She turned on him, her confused and angry feelings making her nasty.

'Was that payment enough for the necklace?' she asked cruelly.

Gabriel stared at her, bitter cynicism shadowing his eyes, and anger closing his face.

'Is that what you think my motives were?' he asked coldly.

Fay gazed at him furiously. He was always so calm, so self-controlled.

'I wouldn't be surprised,' she replied angrily. 'What sort of a man are you, anyway, to make a pass at another man's fiancée?'

Gabriel froze. 'You little bitch!' he gritted. 'You can be sure I'll never touch you again. Forgive me for misinterpreting your responses!'

He strolled indolently from the room, his casual manner belied by his violent slamming of the door.

Fay sank on to the nearest chair and covered her face with her hands. She was trembling from head to toe with reaction and misery. His cutting remarks had struck home and she knew that she had damaged their already shaky relationship beyond repair. She also knew that any motives Gabriel had were good. He had given her flowers and the necklace, collected her birthday cards from the post office, and she had repaid him with insults and contempt. All because he could arouse her, because she loved him and was afraid to betray that love. She could not deny him her love, her body, anything he wanted, and afraid of being considered cheap by him, she had resorted to lies and deceit to keep him away from her. She had certainly succeeded this time, but the knowledge brought only disgust, at her own weakness. She had behaved like the bitch he accused her of being and she could see no way of putting things right. Gabriel had come to mean more to her than anybody in the world, and she could not walk

away from him leaving such bitterness and mis-
understanding between them; she would have to find
the courage to apologise and explain to him.

She dried her eyes and went down to the kitchen in
search of her aunt. She found her, sitting at the kitchen
table, listening to the radio and drinking coffee.

'I thought it wise to keep out of the way while Gabe
gave you your birthday present,' Sophie smiled,
switching off the radio.

'I wish you'd stayed,' Fay said miserably, sinking
into a chair opposite and pouring herself some coffee.

'Why, what happened? Don't tell me you two have
had another row,' Sophie said sympathetically.

Fay nodded.

'But why? That necklace is gorgeous.'

'I know,' Fay agreed. 'It's beautiful and I don't deserve it. Do you know he went to the post office for
my cards this morning?'

'Yes, I know. He told me he thought you ought to
have them on your birthday.' Sophie patted her arm
comfortingly. 'Come—it can't be as bad as all that, not
if he's prepared to do such sweet things for you.'

Fay began to cry again; Sophie's words had touched
something raw and vulnerable inside her.

Sophie grimaced. 'I've said the wrong thing—I'm
sorry.'

'No—no, don't apologise,' Fay hiccoughed noisily.
'It's not your fault. I said such terrible things to him,
Sophie, I don't know how to put things right, and it's
so important that I do.'

Sophie passed her a handkerchief. 'Dry your eyes,
my dear, and let's see if we can sort it out. It really
can't be as bad as you think.'

Fay dried her eyes and blew her nose obediently.
'You think I'm overreacting?' she asked, feeling
calmer.

Sophie shrugged. 'I don't know. What do you think?'

Fay managed a weak smile. 'I think you're right. I am overreacting, that's half the trouble between Gabriel and me, I'm always overreacting!'

'Do you want to tell me what happened just now?'

Fay looked into her aunt's kindly eyes. 'Yes. I don't know what I'd do without you, Sophie. I love you!'

Sophie smiled mistily. Her niece was such a lovely girl, and she would give her any help she could. If Gabriel and Fay needed a little push to get them together, she was more than willing to give it.

Fay began. 'Well, to start with, I've told him that I'm engaged. I know it was stupid, but I think I was almost afraid of him, or myself, and I thought it would keep a good distance between us,' she said miserably. .

'And has it?' Sophie asked mildly.

'It certainly has! I've wanted to tell him the truth, but I can't. He's so honest—oh, I don't know!' Fay rested her head despairingly in her hands.

'You'll have to tell him, Fay, he deserves the truth, you know that,' her aunt said gently.

'Yes. Tonight I tried to give him back the necklace. He refused, of course, and we had a terrible argument—he was very angry. It's never been this bad before,' Fay finished desperately. 'What shall I do?'

'I think you know,' Sophie answered gently, not pushing it.

'I do, but thanks for letting me confide in you. It helps to talk, helps to get things into perspective.'

Sophie smiled. 'Things are liable to get out of proportion when we're all living in each other's pockets. Winter!' she threw up her hands in mock-despair and Fay giggled.

'Shall I make some fresh coffee?' Sophie nodded and Fay got up to put the percolator on the stove.

'Sophie, tell me what you know about Gabriel. I hardly know anything about him—imagine loving somebody you know nothing about!' she laughed, feeling much better.

'You know what matters,' Sophie remarked wisely.

'Tell me the rest, I want to know everything.'

The coffee was ready and Fay sat down and poured it out.

Sophie took a deep breath. 'I first met him through Mary Lewis at the post office. She told me that he was looking for somewhere to buy or rent, so I got in touch with him and offered him the flat upstairs. He was staying with John Baxter and that daughter of his—small wonder he wanted somewhere of his own,' Sophie snorted.

Fay laughed, pitying Lucy Baxter. When Sophie took a dislike to somebody, they did not have a chance!

'Carry on,' she pleaded, sipping her coffee.

'Gabe came to look at the flat, we got on well, so he moved in, and that's it.'

'But what do you know about him?' Fay asked curiously.

'Not much. He's got a house in London and he has no family, I don't think, since his brother died. They were very close and it hit Gabe badly. He's a very successful writer, as you know, and he's rich. I know nothing about his past life, but he's a good man, Fay, honest, intelligent—and of course, he's very attractive,' Sophie finished laughingly.

Fay agreed. 'He told me that he'd been living in Sicily before coming here,' she said thoughtfully.

Sophie nodded. 'I believe he has friends out there— he gets a lot of mail from abroad,' she added wickedly.

Fay yawned. 'I'm so tired.'

'You don't want to take some coffee up to him?' Sophie asked slyly.

Fay shook her head vigorously. 'Not tonight, I couldn't face him. It still hurts too much and I want to work out all the things I have to say. Oh, by the way, I got a note from Sam asking if he can come and visit. If he does, will it be all right?'

'Yes. You don't have to ask, my dear, any of your friends are welcome here.'

Fay got to her feet and stretched wearily. 'Thank you, I appreciate it. I'll just wash up, and then I think I'll go to bed.'

She grabbed a tray and went upstairs to collect the dinner dishes. She stacked them carefully, feeling happier and more confident, having talked over her problems with Sophie. Whistling in an unladylike fashion, she carried the tray back down to the kitchen.

Her aunt was already at the sink, running water, and Fay had to take her by the shoulders and insist that she sat down. Sophie decided to go to bed, so Fay thanked her for the shawl and kissed her goodnight, before packing her firmly off upstairs.

Alone in the kitchen, she washed the dishes quickly and tidied up, laying out the breakfast dishes and preparing things for the following morning. When everything was done, she had no excuse to stay up any longer, so she switched off all the lights and locked the front door, before going upstairs. She washed and undressed and lying in bed, found that she could not sleep. She tossed and turned for about an hour before finally getting up and sitting at the dressing table, where she took Gabriel's necklace out of its box and held it in her hands, sadness filling her heart. It had been a strange birthday, happy and miserable at the same time.

Sighing, she wondered if a hot, milky drink might help her sleep. She pulled on her dressing gown—anything was better than sitting in her room wallowing in misery and self-pity—and made her way downstairs quietly, so as not to disturb anybody. She got as far as the main hall and it was then that she heard noises coming up from the kitchen. Burglars? She picked up a heavy brass ornament from a nearby table and crept down to the kitchen warily, her heart pounding. She pushed open the kitchen door, holding the ornament above her head, and saw Gabriel making coffee.

He turned, looking at her with surprise, eyebrows raised. Fay put the ornament down, feeling foolish.

'I thought you were a thief,' she explained lamely.

'Isn't that what you accuse me of being?' he asked coolly, turning from her again, and continuing with his task of making coffee.

Fay stared miserably at his broad back, trying to pluck up the courage to talk to him. This was a perfect opportunity, so she took a deep breath.

'Gabriel, can I talk to you?'

'Now? Isn't it a little late? Won't it wait until tomorrow?' he asked irritably, his voice still cool, his back still turned to her.

'Yes—no—oh, please, it's important,' she begged, and he turned round, his grim eyes scanning her desperate face.

'Very well,' he agreed with a sigh. 'Do you want some coffee?'

'Yes, please.' She came forward and sat at the table. Gabriel poured coffee for them both and Fay watched him. His tie and jacket were gone, his shirt open low at the neck. His hair was ruffled and he looked tired and strained, his face pale beneath the tan. She had to fight the urge to go to him, hold him, beg for his forgiveness.

He lit a cigarette. 'Do you want one?' he asked, flicking her a cold glance, and Fay nodded eagerly. He held out a lighter and she drew deeply on the cigarette, wondering how to begin. She had no plans for what she would say; she had asked for this chat, on impulse.

'What is it you want to talk about?' Gabriel asked tiredly, expelling smoke from his nostrils in a long stream. He was still angry with her, Fay was sure.

'I wanted to talk about tonight,' she said quietly, looking him straight in the face, her emerald eyes free of deceit. She saw something freeze behind his eyes, but carried on. 'About the things I said to you. . . .'

Gabriel sighed. 'I don't think we have anything to talk about,' he said icily.

Fay stubbed out her cigarette with trembling fingers. She had known it would be difficult, but this was nearly impossible.

'Please, Gabriel,' she began again, 'I have to talk to you, don't make it harder than it already is.'

He shrugged idly. 'Go ahead.'

He was not going to give her any help, and Fay could not blame him.

'The first thing I have to tell you is that I'm not engaged.' It was said, and she felt a great weight lift from her shoulders.

Gabriel's head jerked up and his eyes met hers, cold, grey and cynical.

'Just another lie, eh?' he drawled bitterly, flexing his shoulder muscles wearily, drawing her eyes to the smooth warm skin pressing against the thin fabric of his shirt.

'Yes,' she answered tonelessly, offering no excuse, hoping he would ask.

'Why—in God's name, why?' His question was rough and filled with emotion.

Fay sighed, wondering how to phrase the excuses he wanted, without betraying her love for him.

'I broke off my engagement just before I came to stay here, and when we went for that walk, the first morning, I was confused and a little frightened of you. . . .' Her voice trailed off; she could not explain. Gabriel's fist came down on the table violently, shaking the dishes.

'God, Fay, you knew you had nothing to be frightened of!' he exploded angrily.

Except my own feelings, Fay thought silently.

'You were angry, always so angry with me,' she said weakly, and Gabriel's shoulders sagged.

'I know—I'm sorry,' he said tightly, offering no explanation, and lit another cigarette.

'I've wanted to tell you the truth so often, but the longer I left it, the more difficult it became,' Fay continued with more confidence now, sensing that he was listening to her. 'But I had to tell you tonight, after the cruel and unforgivable things I said. I didn't mean any of them and I'm so sorry—will you forgive me?' she begged.

Gabriel stared at her for a moment, his grey eyes narrow and unreadable. Then he nodded. 'Of course I forgive you,' he said huskily. 'I think we should forget it.'

Fay smiled happily. 'Thank you again for the beautiful necklace. I'll keep it for ever, and treasure it.'

Gabriel smiled too, at her enthusiasm. 'I'm glad,' he said sincerely. 'And I'm glad you told me the truth about your engagement.'

Fay got jerkily to her feet, suddenly feeling out of her depth. He was affecting her deeply, and she wanted to run away.

'Goodnight, and thank you for listening,' she whispered, as she left the kitchen quickly.

'Goodnight, Fay,' Gabriel murmured softly.

She went upstairs slowly, feeling peaceful and contented. She fell asleep the moment her head touched the pillow. At last there were no lies between them.

CHAPTER SIX

THE next afternoon, clad in old jeans and a tee-shirt, Fay cleaned out one of the cupboards beneath the stairs for Sophie. She slipped on an apron and rubber gloves and started while Sophie was taking her afternoon nap. Her aunt had been trying to find something in the cupboard that morning and had given up in despair, so Fay had offered to clean it out. She enjoyed cleaning and the pleasurable sense of achievement it gave her.

The cupboard was crammed full of old furniture, piles of books and magazines and boxes of ornaments and bric-à-brac, that Sophie could not bring herself to give away or throw out, and Fay intended to clean them and sort them out, so that anything her aunt wanted from the cupboard would be on hand. It was a dirty, dusty job and she had not been working long before her face was streaked with dirt and grime, from the numerous times she had brushed her hair out of the way while engrossed in her work.

Halfway through the job, as she was begining to feel pleased with the results that were slowly appearing, the doorbell rang. Muttering crossly, Fay struggled to her feet, wondering who on earth it could be. Sophie had not mentioned that she was expecting anybody, in fact Fay was surprised that anybody had managed to get here, the weather was so bad. She brushed some of the dust from her jeans and went to the door.

The woman who stood outside glanced over Fay disdainfully, a certain malicious amusement in her dark eyes. Fay straightened, and thrust out her chin proudly.

'Can I help you?' she asked coolly, her emerald eyes flashing.

The woman's look made it clear that she doubted so, very much.

'Tell Gabriel I'm here,' she ordered rudely. 'Cecilia Tansley. I'll wait inside.' Without waiting for an invitation, she pushed her way past Fay into the hall.

Fay stood stunned for a second, appalled by the other woman's manners, before gathering her wits together, anger colouring her cheeks.

'Perhaps you'll wait in here,' she managed politely, indicating the lounge, 'and I'll tell Gabriel that you're here.'

The woman strolled languidly into the lounge, looking around her with bored interest, and Fay took the opportunity to examine her carefully. In her early thirties, the woman was tall, slim and chic. She was wearing a pale wool coat, beautifully styled and obviously very expensive, over tweed trousers and knee-length leather boots. A matching leather bag hung from her slim shoulders. Her hair was raven-black, straight and shiny, swinging around her jaw, her eyes were cold and dark, and her beautiful face was expertly made up.

Fay turned away, feeling young and unsophisticated by comparison, and ran upstairs to Gabriel's flat, wondering who on earth the woman was. She knocked on the door. There was no answer, but she could hear the sound of the typewriter within, so she pushed open the door and walked in.

Gabriel was sitting at his desk, working.

'I'm sorry to bother you . . .' she began, trying to ignore the leaping of her heart at the sight of him, dark and virile in an open-necked black shirt and denim jeans.

'Yes?' He looked up from his work reluctantly, irritation creasing his forehead. Then seeing her hurt eyes, 'I'm sorry, Fay, what is it?'

'There's a woman downstairs to see you. Cecilia Tansley.'

'Cecilia? Is she alone?' He frowned.

'I think so. She's waiting in the lounge.'

Gabriel got to his feet, stretching his back and running his hand through the thick darkness of his hair, seeming preoccupied. Fay stared at him, wanting him, and he caught her glance, reaching out to touch her burnished hair with his fingers.

'How are you?' he asked gently.

'Fine,' she shrugged, feeling nervous, and Gabriel laughed.

'What's so funny?' Fay asked aggressively.

'You,' he teased. 'Do you know you've got dirt streaked all over your beautiful face?'

She blushed. 'I don't care.'

They walked downstairs together.

'Shall I make you both some coffee?' she asked as they reached the bottom.

Gabriel smiled. 'That would be fine. Thanks, Fay.'

As he went into the lounge Fay heard Cecilia Tansley's gushing greeting. 'Gabriel darling, it's so good to see you!'

She imagined her in his arms, and felt sick with jealousy.

'Cecilia, is anything wrong?' she heard Gabriel ask, almost immediately.

'I'll tell you everything, darling, after a cup of coffee. I'm dying of thirst! Will that housekeeper, maid or whatever she is, fetch some?'

'Fay is not the housekeeper or the maid,' came Gabriel's curt reply.

Fay did not stay to listen to any more of their conversation, but ran down to the kitchen and began making the coffee, with angry movements. House-keeper, maid indeed! She had disliked Cecilia Tansley on sight, and the thought of her in Gabriel's arms—she obviously knew him well enough—was too much to bear.

She washed her face at the kitchen sink, then having prepared the tray and made the coffee, took it upstairs, wondering what Sophie would have to say about all this.

She walked into the lounge to find Gabriel by the fire and Cecilia Tansley stretched out gracefully on the couch, idly smoking. Their conversation stopped as soon as Fay entered the room.

'Leave it on there,' Cecilia ordered, indicating the small table at her side with a dismissive wave of her hand.

Pursing her lips angrily, Fay moved over to it, fighting the urge to drop the whole tray, scalding hot coffee and all, on the other woman's lap, but Gabriel intervened.

'I've told you, Cecilia, Fay is not the maid,' he repeated coldly, taking the tray from Fay. 'Thank you. Will you stay and have coffee with us?' he asked, smil-ing at her with gentle grey eyes.

'No, I have to get on with my work,' Fay replied loudly, pulling a face at Cecilia.

'Let me introduce you,' Gabriel said politely, a slight smile curving his mouth. 'Fay Drummond, Cecilia Tansley.'

The two women nodded at each other, openly hos-tile, but Fay made an effort for Gabriel's sake.

'How do you do, Miss Tansley.' Cecilia did not even glance at her, and Fay turned away in embarrassment. 'Excuse me,' she mumbled, and left the room, fuming, only remembering just in time to shut the door quietly.

She went back to her work in the cupboard, attacking it with renewed energy born of anger, musing all the while on the situation in the lounge. She was just collecting all the rubbish together, ready to take it downstairs to the boiler, when Gabriel burst from the lounge, his face a mask of fury, his powerful body tense and angry.

'You've left him in the car?' he was asking furiously.

'Gabriel, don't upset yourself, darling, he's asleep, he'll come to no harm,' came Cecilia's soothing and rather patronising reply.

Not deigning to answer, Gabriel stormed past Fay, hardly noticing her, and flung open the front door.

Fay waited with curiosity to see who was in the car, and moments later Gabriel returned, effortlessly carrying a small, sleepy child in his arms. Fay froze, feeling stunned, as he carried the child into the lounge, her mind whirling. How could Cecilia Tansley have left a small child alone in the car, while she sat inside drinking coffee? And who was the child anyway?

She shook her head; it was none of her business, and short of listening at the keyhole she was not going to find out just now. She would take the rubbish downstairs and then take a bath. She certainly needed one, she thought ruefully, glancing down at herself. She was covered with dirt from head to toe. Small wonder that Cecilia Tansley had thought she was a servant! Fay smiled, suddenly seeing the funny side of the encounter that had made her so angry a short time before.

Gabriel came down to the kitchen as she was clearing up. He was still angry, his movements sharp and deliberate, his mouth tight, as he got some milk out of the fridge.

'Can I help?' Fay asked, quelling her urge to ask questions.

'No, but I appreciate your offer,' he said shortly.

'You're very angry,' she remarked mildly, watching him pour the milk into a glass.

'Maybe.'

Fay shook her head at his grim reply and left the room. She did not want to get involved with Gabriel's anger, she had experienced too much of it already.

She ran a hot bath, pouring in handfuls of scented bath crystals, and then soaked herself for an hour, until at last the water cooling drove her out. She dried her hair quickly and dressed in rust-coloured velvet trousers and a toning silk blouse, after applying a light make-up. She felt the need to look good, especially with Cecilia Tansley in the house. Would the other woman be staying for dinner?

Her worst fears were confirmed when she went downstairs to prepare dinner. Standing in the hall were three pale leather suitcases. Fay went down to the kitchen to find her aunt peeling vegetables, a resigned look on her face.

'You know?' Fay asked.

Sophie nodded.

'Who is she?'

'I've no idea. Gabriel will be down any moment, perhaps we'll know then.' Fay began washing the vegetables.

'Do you think the child is Gabriel's?' she asked, voicing her worst fear.

Sophie shrugged. 'Gabriel introduced me to Miss Tansley and the boy, he didn't say who they were. By the way, thanks for cleaning out that cupboard under the stairs, I hardly recognise it.'

'I was glad to do it, Sophie, you know that.'

At that moment Gabriel walked into the kitchen and conversation stopped. Fay smiled at him, unable to stop herself, and he smiled back.

He went to Sophie, taking both her hands. 'I'm sorry Sophie, I had no idea they were coming—if I had, I would have warned you, sorted something out. I don't want to put you to any extra trouble, so I'll book them into a hotel. . . .'

Sophie cut across him sternly.

'You'll do no such thing! Any friends of yours are welcome here. There's plenty of room and I insist that they stay, they'll be no extra trouble. We'll sort out some rooms after dinner,' she said firmly. 'Don't argue, Gabe!' she warned with twinkling eyes.

Gabriel knew when he was beaten. He bent down and kissed Sophie's forehead.

'Thank you,' he said quietly.

'If Miss Tansley would like a bath before dinner, will you show her where everything is?'

Gabriel smiled. 'You're an angel, Sophie!'

'Get away with you, out of my kitchen, while we get dinner,' Sophie mock-scolded him out of the kitchen as Fay watched, realising that her aunt was glad to have people staying in the house. How lonely it must be for her, all alone in this big house.

'Yes, I get lonely,' Sophie admitted, reading Fay's thoughts, as she put the potatoes into a pan. 'This house can be very big and empty,' she said wryly.

Fay laughed. 'By the look of Cecilia Tansley, we're going to have a good deal of extra work.'

'It will be nice to have a child in the house again, though,' Sophie replied, seeing the good side of things, as always.

As Fay changed for dinner, later, her thoughts returned to the child. Gabriel cared for him, that was obvious. Was Cecilia Tansley his mistress? Fay dismissed the thought from her mind painfully, unable to bear it. The thought of that cold, dark woman lying in his arms filled her with despair and misery.

'Oh, Gabriel,' she whispered sadly, filled with a sudden longing to be near him, as she slid into the black silk dress she had chosen for dinner. She took Gabriel's necklace from its box and fastened it around her neck. Slipping her feet into high-heeled black sandals, she was ready, aware of how poised and sophisticated she looked, and the knowledge gave her much-needed confidence. Cecilia Tansley would be a hostile adversary, and Fay needed all the confidence she could muster.

She strolled slowly downstairs, somehow unwilling to face everybody. Deep inside she felt like crying and she wanted to go to Cecilia Tansley and warn her away from Gabriel, to tell her to leave him alone, to go away. Pulling herself together, she fought against the jealousy threatening to consume her.

She went down to the kitchen to check the meal, admitting to herself that it was only an excuse, a putting-off of the time when she would have to go into the lounge. The back door was open, the freezing cold night air cooling the kitchen. Fay went over to close it and saw Gabriel standing outside, alone. He seemed to be staring into space, his tall, powerful body perfectly still, an air of anguish about him.

'Gabriel . . .?' she whispered, stepping out into the cold night, and touching his arm shyly, afraid that he might be ill. He turned to her, his grey eyes tormented, and she looked up into his face, her concern mirrored in her emerald eyes, and gentle mouth.

'You're wearing the necklace,' he said softly, as if he were surprised.

Fay smiled. 'Yes—it's beautiful.' He looked at her for a moment, searching her face with clouded eyes.

'Oh God, Fay,' he groaned suddenly, 'hold me.' His voice was rough with an aching intensity that turned Fay's heart over. She recognised his need, just to be close to somebody, and slid her arms around his waist, closing her eyes as his arms came around her, crushing her close to him. She held him tightly, giving him her comfort as he buried his strong face in the softness of her hair. She felt afraid for him, absurdly protective, as they clung together. Something was tearing him apart, and because she loved him it was tearing her apart too.

Then he put her away from him gently, holding both her hands in his, as they stood together staring into each other's eyes.

'They'll be wondering where we are,' she said softly, not caring. He shrugged carelessly, but took her arm and they walked into the house.

'Fay——' he began, but she stopped him, shaking her head.

'Don't say anything, please.' She felt near to tears and very sensitive. Gabriel tilted up her face with strong, hard fingers.

'Okay.' He kissed her, his hard mouth brushing hers briefly, then he was gone.

Fay sat down at the table feeling deeply shaken and weak. Something pure and profound had passed between them outside and she wanted to keep the feeling with her as long as she could.

At last, realising that she would have to go upstairs and join everyone in the lounge before dinner, she took a deep breath and got to her feet.

Sophie was handing out drinks, doing her best to be polite to Cecilia Tansley, who was looking quite stunning in a tight scarlet dress, beautifully made, which left little of her lissom, perfect figure to the imagination. Gabriel was sitting, relaxed by the fire, smoking, the mood that had driven him into Fay's arms obviously gone, as he made Cecilia laugh, a cool, tinkling laughter that reminded Fay of crushed ice.

Fay's eyes rested on him for a long moment before making her way over to the drinks tray, to pour herself a sherry. She sat by Sophie, who was chatting to Cecilia and Gabriel, and tried to keep out of the conversation. Her aunt was looking splendid and very dignified in a beige evening dress, and even Cecilia Tansley seemed impressed.

There was no sign of the little boy.

'Has the child gone to bed?' she asked Sophie quietly.

Her aunt nodded. 'He was very tired. I've put him in the room next to yours—I hope you don't mind. I'm afraid he might have nightmares, and I don't suppose she'll hear,' she nodded in the direction of Cecilia Tansley.

Fay followed her nod, her mouth tightening unconsciously as she watched the other woman leaning towards Gabriel, to whisper something to him, something that made him smile. She turned away.

Sophie was talking. 'You know what my hearing is like——'

'Sorry, Sophie, I was miles away. What did you say?'

'I was just explaining about Danny—the little boy,' she expanded, seeing Fay's confusion. 'I would have put him next to me, but I wouldn't hear him if he did cry out in the night.'

'That's fine, I don't mind, honestly. I like children,' Fay replied consolingly. 'Do you know how long they're staying?'

'No idea. How is the dinner?'

'I'll go and check.' Fay got to her feet eagerly, glad of the chance of escape, her eyes straying to the couple only a few feet away.

Sophie detained her. 'There's no need, my dear, I'll go.'

Fay shook her head. 'I want to,' she replied almost desperately.

Sophie followed the direction of her niece's sad eyes, and let her go.

Everything was ready in the kitchen, and piling the serving dishes on to a tray, Fay took them upstairs to the dining room. She announced dinner, then returned to the kitchen for the meat, tender roast lamb. Dinner passed slowly. Fay ate mechanically, refusing to be drawn into the conversation by Gabriel, who had managed to put everybody at ease, with his amusing and charming chat. Fay watched as even Sophie succumbed to him. Cecilia Tansley was hanging on his every word, her dark eyes glowing with undisguised and feverish desire. She wanted him, just as Fay did, but she had a great deal more beauty and cunning.

Gabriel's clear grey eyes rested on Fay many times during the meal. He was aware of her awkward and unfriendly behaviour and she knew that he was trying hard to include her. But she refused to be drawn, her mind filled with the child who lay upstairs, and the woman who sat beside him, and endless questions. Was Cecilia Tansley Gabriel's lover? she asked herself for at least the tenth time that day, before making an effort to pull herself together. What was the point of flaying herself with painful questions? She knew nothing for sure.

Fay insisted on making the coffee, and bringing up the chocolate gâteau, made by Sophie that morning, and the cheese, and when at last the meal was over she told Sophie to go and sit in the lounge with Cecilia and Gabriel while she washed the dishes. The thought of having to spend the evening watching the man she loved being captivated by the beautiful Miss Tansley made Fay's head ache worse than it did already. Sophie was concerned as she helped Fay to clear the table.

'Fay, you go next door and let me do these,' she insisted.

'Please, Sophie.' Fay was at the end of her patience, and had to force herself to speak calmly. 'I don't want to sit in there with them, I have a splitting headache. Please let me wash up.' Sophie gave in.

Fay washed up slowly, concentrating on each plate carefully, in an effort to take her mind off things. She did not hear Gabriel come into the room, until he stood beside her, making her jump.

'Let me help,' he said, watching her profile as she worked.

'No,' Fay replied shortly, not looking at him.

'What's the matter?' He was easy and relaxed, his eyes warm and clear as he looked at her.

'Nothing. I don't want any help. Go away, please,' she said steadily.

Gabriel sighed, running his finger lightly down her cheek, making her flinch, making her want him.

'As you wish,' he said quietly. 'You can't avoid me for ever.'

He left the kitchen.

Fay finished her work. She would go to bed. But first she had to make her excuses and say goodnight. She walked into the lounge, almost stopping dead in her tracks at the sight before her. The radio was on and Cecilia was pulling Gabriel to his feet, begging him to dance with her. He was polite and reluctant. Her polished nails slid over his broad shoulders, her dark head came against his chest. Fay's eyes met his, and his darkened angrily at the naked contempt on her face.

Fay murmured her excuses to Sophie, dragging her gaze from the dancing couple with difficulty, pain and jealousy squeezing her heart, making her breathless, then she left the room, the image remaining in front of her blind, unseeing eyes. She ran upstairs, unable to control her tears, and had just reached her room when a hand closed on her shoulder and she was spun around to face Gabriel.

'What is it?' he demanded grimly. 'Are you ill?'

'Let me go!' she snapped, shivering at his touch, burning through the thin silk of her dress.

'Tell me,' he repeated harshly, his hooded eyes dark on her bent head.

It was futile to deny him, he would not let her go until he had his answer.

'I've got a headache,' she said truthfully, trying to wriggle from his grasp.

'And it's so bad as to make you cry like this?' he questioned, clearly not believing her.

Fay nodded, not trusting herself to answer.

Gabriel groaned frustratedly, letting her go, and then they heard the cry—the cry of a frightened child awoken in the night by a bad dream.

They both moved automatically to the next room, and Fay wiped her eyes as she switched on the light. The little boy was sitting up in bed, his small pale face wet with frightened tears. As Fay looked at him, the first time she had seen him properly, any hopes that she might have had for her and Gabriel were dashed for ever. The child was his. Danny had dark hair, and the clear grey eyes of his father; the resemblance was startling.

Gabriel went to the child and picked him up, cradling him gently in his arms, his strong face warm with love as he wiped away the little boy's tears and soothed him with softly spoken words. Danny clung to him trustingly and Fay watched with tears in her eyes again.

'Shall I make him a hot drink? It might help him to sleep again,' she said huskily, feeling almost an intruder on this tender scene.

'Would you?' Gabriel asked, turning to her, his clear eyes still gentle and warm.

Fay nodded, her heart aching, and fled from the room.

She warmed some milk, and added a spoonful of honey and a sprinkling of cinnamon, then carried it upstairs carefully in a child's mug, one of Judy's, that Sophie had kept for sentimental reasons, patterned with rabbits. Perhaps it would cheer Danny up, and help him to sleep.

When she got back to the bedroom, Gabriel had put the boy back into his bed and was sitting on the edge of it, telling him a story. Fay handed him the mug and began to walk away.

'Wait, Fay, please,' Gabriel halted her.

'I'll wait outside,' she promised huskily. 'Goodnight, Danny,' she smiled gently at the child.

'G'night,' came the squeaky reply. She stood outside the bedroom waiting for Gabriel. She could not have stayed inside, it was a private time between Gabriel and Danny—and besides, it hurt too much. Eventually Gabriel came out, switching off the light, the rabbit mug hanging from his fingers.

'He's asleep,' he said softly, and Fay smiled.

They stood together, almost touching. 'I wanted to thank you for taking such care,' he indicated the mug, and Fay blushed brightly.

'It was nothing, just that I remember how awful warm milk tastes on its own.'

Gabriel smiled at her self-deprecation. 'It was caring, and I appreciate it,' he said firmly.

Fay bowed her head, feeling embarrassed. 'He's a lovely child, anybody would want to help him,' she said haltingly.

'Yes, he is a lovely child.' Gabriel sounded distant.

Fay looked up at him, hearing the sadness in his voice. Was he regretting the fact that he had not married Cecilia Tansley? She did not want to be involved, she had been hurt enough already.

'Goodnight.' She opened her bedroom door and went inside, not listening to hear if he answered.

As she lay in bed, waiting for sleep to claim her, the tears welled up in her eyes again and she wept for what she had lost, what she had never had.

Late the next morning Fay was having some coffee in the lounge when Cecilia Tansley strolled in and sat down gracefully opposite her.

'Is there any coffee left in the pot?' she asked, her voice quite friendly.

Fay looked up at her sharply, wondering rather suspiciously at the other woman's friendly tone. Cecilia Tansley had not even managed to be polite up to now. Chiding herself for this unfounded suspicion, Fay smiled warily. 'Yes, shall I pour you a cup?'

'Please.' Cecilia crossed her slim legs and lit a cigarette. Fay glanced at her again as she passed the cup. Cecilia was looking stunning in a black wool dress that complemented her dark colouring. Discreet gold jewellery hung from her wrists and ears, and she looked beautiful and expensive—the exact opposite to me, Fay thought wryly, examining her own battered jeans and practical but rather boring sweater. With a further shock, she saw Cecilia smile as she began to speak.

'This really is a lovely old house. Do you live here, Fay? I hope you don't mind me calling you Fay—and you must call me Cecilia.'

Fay fought the urge to laugh. So this was the reason for Cecilia's friendliness! She had deliberately sought her out in an effort to discover her position in the house, and no doubt her attitude to Gabriel. Was she really so desperate for him that she had sunk to being so obvious? And did she really see Fay as competition?

'No, I don't live here. Sophie is my aunt and I'm just having a holiday here,' she replied, smiling at Cecilia's obvious relief.

'Have you been here long?' Cecilia managed to soften her interrogation with another smile.

'Just over three weeks now. It's a wonderfully relaxing place. Are you planning to stay long?' Two can play at this game, Fay thought, pleased with her innocent question.

Cecilia shrugged carelessly, stubbing out her cigarette. 'As long as is necessary,' she replied significantly, then, 'Do tell me, what do you think of Gabriel?' Her dark eyes narrowed in challenge on Fay's pale face.

She certainly gets straight to the point, Fay thought with amusement. 'I like him,' she replied noncommittally, deliberately vague.

Cecilia smiled again, obviously pleased with Fay's casual reply.

'Show me a woman who doesn't,' she said, her eyes filled with secrets that Fay longed to know.

'You're close friends—you and Gabriel?' Fay stared at the other woman curiously, painfully wondering at her knowledge of him.

'Very close,' Cecilia answered smugly. Fay was no threat to her, but it would do no harm to secure her own position, to make sure. 'I've known him for many years now—he came to our house in Sicily very often, he and his brother Alex.' She let her voice become reminiscent. 'They were such good times!'

Fay stared at her with dislike. She and Gabriel had obviously enjoyed a long and close relationship, and she did not want to know about it.

'Do you work, Cecilia?' she asked, changing the subject, not really interested in the answer.

Cecilia arched her thin perfect eyebrows. 'I'm a photographic model,' she replied haughtily. 'I'm surprised you don't know my face—I'm very well known in Italy.'

Fay suppressed another giggle, marvelling at Cecilia's arrogance.

'It must be fascinating work,' she managed in reply.

'It is—in fact that's how I first met Alex. He was the photographer on one of my assignments, wildly attractive, although of course once I'd met Gabriel. . . .' She allowed her voice to trail off suggestively, intending to leave Fay in no doubt that Gabriel was her property. She had waited too long for him, far too long to tolerate any interference from this pale young girl with the beautiful eyes. Gabriel must not be interested in her—must not receive any encouragement from her. Alex's death had been almost opportune, giving Cecilia her chance to seek Gabriel out again, to use Danny to force him into the position she had failed to put him in herself. He would not reject her again.

She got slowly to her feet and smoothed the black dress over her slender hips, flashing Fay a cold triumphant smile.

'Excuse me, Fay, I must see Gabriel before lunch.' She strolled from the room, leaving Fay miserable and alone with the distinct impression that she had been warned off.

CHAPTER SEVEN

'SAM!' Fay's voice was incredulous as she gazed at the man in front of her.

'Didn't you get my card?' Sam asked with a smile, his eyes looking over her and the small boy who was clinging to her hand.

'Yes. I don't know why I'm surprised to see you—come in.'

Despite the bitterness and the hurt between them, Fay felt glad to see him. She stood back from the front door and let him in, looking at him, young and strong and familiar, in old jeans and a sheepskin coat, so different from the tall dark man who haunted her days and nights so ruthlessly.

Sam kissed her affectionately and Fay remembered Danny, who was staring up at them with interest.

'Sam, this is Danny, and Danny, this is Sam, my friend.'

Sam knelt down, laughing, and shook Danny's small hand. Danny smiled at him warily and said hello, and Fay watched, unable to stop herself smiling. Sam had a way with children, probably with coming from such a large family.

'Come into the lounge and sit by the fire—you must be freezing,' she laughed, leading the way.

The lounge was empty and Danny ran over to the coffee table, found his drawing book and crayons and began colouring. Fay watched him with loving eyes. Over the past two days she had become very fond of him. His resemblance to Gabriel and his quiet, loving nature had endeared him to her. She turned her attention back to Sam.

'Take your coat off,' she ordered. 'Would you like some coffee? I've just made some.'

Sam nodded. 'I've missed you, Fay,' he said quietly.

'I've missed you too,' she replied honestly. 'But you haven't come to . . .?'

'No, I just want to set things straight between us, and I couldn't wait any longer,' Sam smiled boyishly.

His impatience had always been a problem, and Fay shook her head, suddenly feeling much older than him, even though they were the same age.

'I'll get the coffee, then we can talk.' She took his coat. 'Do you want something to eat? Will you be staying? Oh, Sam, I am glad to see you!' She reached up and kissed him, not giving him the chance to answer her breathless questions. He held her away from him, laughing into her eyes, and at that moment Gabriel walked into the room. He took in the scene before him with dark, narrowed eyes, Fay and Sam laughing together, their arms around each other, and Fay saw his mouth tighten.

'Excuse me, I was looking for Cecilia,' he said coldly, politely, and shut the door violently.

Fay flinched at his cold anger and Sam stared at her curiously.

'Who's that?' he asked.

'Gabriel Winter,' Fay replied miserably, wishing that she did not love him, wishing that he did not have the power to hurt her with a cold glance.

'The writer?' Sam had recognised the name.

'Yes. I'll get the coffee. Did you say you wanted something to eat?' she asked, changing the subject; she did not want to talk about Gabriel.

'You didn't give me the chance,' Sam laughed. 'No, I'm not hungry.'

Fay went down to the kitchen slowly, still feeling

hurt, to find Gabriel sitting at the table, smoking. Her heart leapt, but she ignored him, as she switched on the percolator and set about making some chocolate for Danny. But the heavy silence and Gabriel's brooding eyes, watching her every movement, unnerved her and she had to speak.

'Can I have a cigarette, please?' she asked in a high, loud voice.

He lit one for her, handing it to her, and coming to stand behind her, so close that she could feel his breath in her hair.

Fay drew on her cigarette shakily, fighting her overwhelming desire to turn and go into his arms. Instead she moved away. 'Do you want some coffee?' she asked, feeling sure that he must hear her pounding heart.

'No,' Gabriel replied uncompromisingly. 'Who is he?'

'Why were you so rude?' she parried, angry with him.

His grey eyes glittered as he moved towards her. 'It's Sam. I told you about him,' Fay said with a breathless rush, feeling almost frightened, as he towered over her.

'Your ex-fiancé,' he remarked cruelly. Fay felt the sting of salt tears in her eyes, at something in his voice.

'You can be a real swine sometimes,' she accused brokenly.

'You'll do well to remember that,' Gabriel warned harshly, a muscle jerking in his jaw.

Then he was gone, leaving Fay trembling and shaken. She piled up the tray, adding some thin slices of fruit cake, and then took it upstairs, her movements mechanical and automatic, as she wondered about Gabriel's angry behaviour.

Sam was colouring with Danny as she entered the lounge, but he jumped up and took the tray from her, smiling. Fay pulled the curtains together and switched on the lamps, as Sam poured the coffee. Then they sat by the fire with Danny on Fay's knee, eating his cake and drinking his chocolate with serious concentration on his small face, and Fay and Sam began to talk.

Sam started. 'I wanted to apologise, love, for giving you such a hard time when you left. It was just hurt pride, I guess.'

'No, I was cruel, I didn't know how to tell you that I couldn't marry you without hurting you. I didn't even try to be kind,' Fay said regretfully, remembering the row.

Sam shook his head in disagreement.

'It wasn't your fault. I've had plenty of time to think things out and I know now that it would have been a disaster if we'd married. We've always been too close.'

'Yes, we're brother and sister,' Fay agreed.

'I still love you, Fay,' Sam admitted gently.

'And I love you,' Fay replied. 'And I'm so glad that we haven't lost each other, that you came here to sort things out. When I got your note I was worried,' she admitted honestly, 'but I was going to come and see you when I got back to London anyway.'

They drank their coffee in companionable silence, knowing each other's minds, having no need to talk. Danny fell asleep on Fay's knee, after his drink, the firelight bright on his small sad face, and she held him gently, stroking his hair, loving him with anguish.

Sam smiled at Fay, his young strong face peaceful.

'Will we always be this close?' he asked wonderingly.

'I hope so, it means so much to me,' Fay replied dreamily.

'Looking back, I don't know how we could have

thought of getting married, it would have spoilt all this,' Sam laughed. 'We didn't think—I didn't think, I'm sorry.'

'It wasn't just you, Sam, it was me as well, and family pressure, and—who knows? Is it really sorted out?' she asked, looking into his eyes, green like her own. She saw that it was. There was no anger, no bitterness, no hurt in his eyes, only love, brotherly love and happiness. He was completely uncomplicated, so different from Gabriel.

'Will you stay for a few days, if it's all right with Sophie?' she asked, wanting him to.

'Yes, I'd like to.'

As if on cue, Sophie came in.

'Sam! How lovely to see you,' she exclaimed, shaking his hand. 'You will be staying, I hope?'

'Thank you, I will.'

'At this rate, the house will be packed with people,' Fay remarked laughingly. 'The coffee is still hot, will you have a cup, Sophie?'

Her aunt settled down on the couch, and they spent the rest of the afternoon chatting.

Dinner was quiet. Gabriel and Cecilia had gone out to dinner and Fay spent a miserable evening, knowing that they were together. She put Danny to bed, reading him a story before he went to sleep. She watched him as he slept. He was such a beautiful child, how could Cecilia treat him so casually? He needed love so badly, and yet she hardly seemed to spend any time with him. The whole situation was unclear. Why hadn't Gabriel married Cecilia and given Danny his name? He loved the boy, Fay knew for sure. It puzzled her.

She went downstairs to join Sophie and Sam. She had to put it out of her mind or she would go mad. The evening passed quickly and pleasantly, and for once Fay felt relaxed. Her nerves were always highly-strung when Gabriel was about, it was like living on a knife-edge. They all retired to bed early. Sam in particular was tired after his journey. The snow was still holding off, surprisingly, and Lambrigg House had still not been cut off, although the roads were still very dangerous.

Fay looked in on Danny again, before she went to bed. He was sleeping soundly, but she left her door ajar, in case he cried out in the night.

As she lay in bed, her thoughts, as ever, turned to Gabriel, as she wondered again at his cruelty that afternoon. If only she did not love him!

She woke in the night, suddenly, and lay still for a moment, wondering what had woken her, then she heard Danny crying. She jumped out of bed and grabbed her dressing-gown, not bothering to put it on, in her haste to be with him. She found him sitting up in bed, crying, and she took him in her arms and comforted him.

'Don't go away,' he kept repeating through his tears, his fear obvious.

'I won't, Danny, I won't,' Fay whispered, rocking him gently, reassuring him. He took a long time to quieten, his small arms tight around her neck, and she held him, anger seething inside her. Cecilia should be holding him, comforting him. It was tearing at Fay's heart as she became more emotionally involved with Gabriel's son, knowing as she did that there was nothing between Gabriel and herself except her love.

She must have fallen asleep, still holding Danny, because she woke with a start, the next morning, to find Gabriel standing over them—she and Danny still holding each other, a curious expression in his grey eyes. Fay lay still for a moment, collecting her thoughts and remembering the events of the previous night.

Embarrassment washed over her as she realised her

position, also realising that her flimsy nightdress left
her practically naked, a fact testified by Gabriel's insolent eyes, as they slid the length of her body as she
watched, taking in her soft, rounded breasts, only half
covered by the thin gauzy material, and her slim bare
legs. His gaze became hooded as it returned to her
flushed face and, expecting censure, Fay lifted her chin
defiantly, surprised by the gentle amusement her
action produced.

She carefully untangled Danny's arms from around
her neck, and looked round for her dressing-gown,
which she distinctly remembered bringing in with her.
It was on the floor, and even as her eyes fell on it,
Gabriel reached down and picked it up.

Fay looked up at him fearfully. He was fully dressed
in black trousers and a black shirt, dark clothes that
gave him a lean and virile menacing look, that made
his eyes silver-bright, and only served to emphasise
Fay's near nakedness.

She could not tell whether or not he was angry, but
she had to find out. 'Can I have my dressing-gown,
please?' she asked in a small, cool voice.

'Come and get it,' Gabriel taunted softly, his eyes
suddenly dark with what Fay realised, with a shock of
tingling sensation, was desire. She did not move, but
lay on the bed, her heart pounding as she tried to
clarify the situation she found herself in. She ran a
hand confusedly through her tousled auburn hair,
unaware that her unconsciously sensual movements
brought Gabriel's molten gaze back to the fullness of
her breasts. She swallowed nervously, wanting him,
even as she sought her escape, but it was difficult to
move with the languorous weakness that flooded her
body. She must try.

Danny was sleeping peacefully and Fay carefully
shifted her weight to the other side of the bed and got

to her feet, checking that she had not disturbed him.

Gabriel was still watching her hungrily, holding her dressing-gown with idle hands.

'How long ...?' she began, wanting to know how long he had been watching them sleep, but he gave her no chance to finish, reading her mind easily.

'About half an hour,' he replied softly. 'Does that worry you?'

Fay could not speak, the words were sticking in her throat. She had to get away.

'Can I have my dressing-gown?' she repeated, her voice breathless and weak. The tension stretched between them and around them, like strong ropes. Gabriel stood still, strong and unmoving, blocking her exit from the small bedroom, his silver eyes never leaving her face.

'I told you—come and get it,' he said again, his voice deadly, soft and husky. Fay shivered uncontrollably.

'Please, Gabriel. . . .' she begged, not knowing what she begged for.

Gabriel ignored her, reaching out and touching her throat with strong caressing fingers, heightening the tense web of desire that was spinning around them. Fay turned her head away, knocking his fingers from her throat, her eyes on Danny, still sleeping peacefully, unaware of what was happening in his room. Danny— Gabriel's son. Feeling sick, she turned back to Gabriel and tried to push past him, uncaring of the close contact. She pushed at the hard wall of his chest, but it was futile.

'Let me past!' she said angrily, her green eyes flashing.

Gabriel put a warning finger over her lips, then before she realised what was happening, he swung her into his arms and carried her into her own room. He deposited her ungently on the bed and arched over her.

She stared up into his lean face, her heart beating so fast she feared it might burst.

'I want you, Fay—dear God, I want you,' Gabriel said slowly, his molten silver eyes intent on her mouth. 'Tell me that Sam has never been your lover—I want to hear you say it.'

Fay licked her dry lips, with no thought of denying him.

'Sam has never been my lover,' she repeated obediently, honestly, shivering at the triumph she saw in his eyes as she spoke.

Gabriel lowered his head, his mouth touching hers exploringly, and Fay could not fight him any longer. She needed him. His possessive hands slid beneath her thin nightdress to find the soft scented skin beneath, and she was weak with her need for him to touch her, unable to resist him, not wanting to anyway.

She reached up to cradle his face in her hands as their mouths moved against each other, desperately. Gabriel was breathing hard.

'Touch me,' he groaned, his mouth urgent against her bare shoulder.

Fay reached for his chest, undoing his shirt with trembling fingers, sliding her hands over the warm hair-roughened skin beneath, with a deep sigh of satisfaction. Gabriel shuddered as she touched him, his heart pounding beneath her stroking fingers. His arms came around her then, moulding her close to the hard length of his body, his hands moving with ever-increasing urgency over her slender body.

The sound of raised voices outside the bedroom door broke over them, stiffening them both. Gabriel swore angrily, violently, his savage words bringing Fay to her senses, as he got to his feet, buttoning his shirt with unsteady fingers. He was breathing deeply, regaining control, and she stared at him, her emerald eyes still glazed with desire.

Gabriel groaned. 'Don't look at me like that, I can't stand it!'

Fay smiled provocatively, reaching out to touch his lean thigh, feeling the tightening of his muscles beneath her fingers.

The voices had gone, and Gabriel moved cautiously to the door.

'I'll have to go,' he said reluctantly, huskily. 'Oh, Fay, it's tearing me apart to leave you like this, but if Sophie. . . .' He bit off his words with a harsh epithet.

'Go,' Fay said softly, smiling at him. He was thinking of her and she loved him for it.

A moment after he had gone, she heard Cecilia's voice on the landing. Had she seen Gabriel coming from her room? Perhaps she had, because they began to argue. Fay put her hands over her ears, and buried herself beneath the bedclothes, loath to hear what they were saying and wishing herself a thousand miles away.

About half an hour later she got up. The landing was deserted and peeping into Danny's room, she found it empty. She took a cold shower, the water hitting her aching and overheated body like ice needles, then dried herself vigorously, feeling a little better. She dressed quickly, trying to dispel the misery that blanketed her thoughts, and went downstairs.

Fortunately the kitchen was also empty. She made some coffee and lit a cigarette, the thought of food making her feel sick. Hearing voices outside, she went to the window, to see Danny and Gabriel playing outside in the snow. She stood very still, drawn to them as she watched. Gabriel was laughing, absorbed and totally relaxed, all the dark emotion so often apparent in him gone, as he swung the little boy in his arms.

Fay looked at him carefully, at his gentle loving eyes,

at his obvious happiness. Then her gaze slid to Danny, so like Gabriel, his small face shining as he shouted and screamed with delight. They were both supremely happy in each other's company—a strong bond of love seemed to stretch between them, and Fay's emotions were mixed as she looked on. It was touching and beautiful to see them together, it seemed right somehow, but it also brought a poignant sadness and many unanswered questions, and a surge of unknown emotion so strong that she felt she would explode. But still she continued watching them with clouded eyes until Gabriel hoisted the little boy on to his shoulders and they walked away towards the woods, still laughing together. Why was it so easy to love them both?

Fay made up her mind at that moment that she would return to London as soon as possible. She would go back with Sam; he was only staying a few days. With Cecilia and Danny here, it was impossible for her to stay, loving Gabriel as she did. As the mother of his child, Cecilia had a claim on him, and Fay would not come between them. She sat down at the table again and poured another cup of coffee, wondering what her life would be like without him.

Sam found her after lunch, strolling into the lounge where she was sitting reading, feeling miserable. Danny was holding his hand.

'Hi, I've been looking for you,' he said brightly.

''Lo, Fay!' shouted Danny, running over to take her hand.

'Hello, darling,' Fay smiled at the little boy, and kissed the top of his head. He looked sweet in tiny dungarees and a brightly-striped woollen jumper.

'Where have you been all morning?' Sam asked complainingly, his eyes teasing.

'In my room, mostly,' Fay replied vaguely, shutting her book. 'What are you two going to do this afternoon?' she questioned, forcing herself to sound jolly.

Sam smiled, seeing through her, but not mentioning it.

'We want you to come and help us build a snowman on the lawn, don't we, Danny?'

'Yes! Yes!' Danny jumped up and down with excitement, tugging at Fay's arm, his grey eyes shining.

'Okay.' Fay felt cheered up despite herself. 'Let's get our coats and boots, and go outside.'

Danny ran off immediately to get his coat and Fay looked at Sam.

'Cecilia was tired,' he said wryly, 'so I offered to take Danny for the afternoon.'

'And Gabriel, what's his excuse?' Fay asked sharply.

'He's gone into town to get something for Sophie. He wanted to take Danny, but Cecilia refused.' Sam explained the situation that had arisen over lunch, as they got their coats. 'He was angry, it was obvious.'

Fay looked at him, hoping he would not notice her flushed face. 'He's got a very short temper,' she explained, grimacing.

'You've suffered?' Sam laughed, ruffling her hair.

Fay nodded. 'Sam, do you find Cecilia attractive?'

He considered for a moment. 'I guess she's quite beautiful, but very cold. I think she could destroy any man who loved her,' he answered seriously. He hugged her. 'You're more beautiful, and you're warm and gentle,' he said against her ear.

Fay giggled, and pushed him away, used to his extravagant compliments. 'Let's find Danny.'

They found him pulling on his wellingtons with difficulty. Fay knelt before him, fastening his coat, tying his scarf and putting on his gloves and hat, then Sam carried him downstairs, while Fay went in search of some clothes for their snowman. It was her second snowman this winter, she thought with a smile.

The snowman took ages to build, the work being interspersed with snowball fights, and lots of laughter, but finally he was ready, a huge round snowman over six feet tall. Sam lifted Danny up so that the child could stick the pieces of coal in for the eyes and mouth, and the carrot nose. They put on the scarf and hat, then went in search of twigs for arms. Fay had found an old umbrella which she hung over the snowman's twig arm. He was complete, and they stood back laughing together.

'What shall we call him, Danny?'

'Danny—like me,' the little boy answered immediately, so Fay took pieces of coal and stuck them on the front of the snowman to form the word DANNY.

Sam lifted Danny on to his shoulders and put his arm around Fay's waist, and they stood together, admiring their afternoon's work. It was quite magnificent and Danny was excited, bouncing up and down on Sam's shoulders. They were like a family, Fay thought unhappily. Anybody watching them would think that she and Sam were married, and that Danny was their child. She closed her eyes painfully, wishing that Danny was her child, hers and Gabriel's.

Sam was singing a carol, even though it was long after Christmas, and Danny was singing too, so Fay joined in, their voices loud and happy in the quiet of the dark afternoon.

The Land Rover came slowly up the drive and Fay ignored it, even though her heart raced away at the sight of it. But Danny had seen it too, and insisting that Sam put him down, he ran over to it and dragged Gabriel back to them, chattering excitedly all the while. Fay watched as they came towards her, the tall, strong man, and the little boy—so alike. Their eyes met, Gabriel's narrowed and enigmatic, Fay's wide and sad.

Gabriel admired the snowman, then swung Danny into his arms, his eyes on Sam's arm around Fay. She met his brooding glance with a defiant smile, moving closer to Sam, and watching Gabriel's mouth tighten with sadistic pleasure.

'I'll have to start dinner,' she murmured.

Sam nodded, and they walked back to the house, leaving Danny and Gabriel playing in the snow together.

Sam watched her carefully as he helped to prepare the curry Fay had decided on for dinner.

'Do you think Gabriel loves Cecilia?' Fay asked, speaking her mind.

Sam shrugged. 'Does it matter?' he asked, still watching her.

'It does for Danny,' she replied sharply.

'Danny is definitely Gabriel's son?'

'You only have to look at them!' Fay snapped. 'I'm sorry,' she apologised.

Sam put his arm around her.

'You love him,' he stated flatly. Fay stared into his face and knew that she could not lie to him.

'Yes, I love him,' she replied miserably. 'And I know that he doesn't love me, we don't even get on with each other.' She caught the sadness in Sam's eyes. 'You're upset.'

Sam smiled weakly. 'A little,' he admitted. 'I've lost you.'

'Oh, Sam, I still love you, you know that.'

They both turned at the sound of the kitchen door, shutting quietly.

'Who was it, did you see?'

Sam walked over to the door, opened it and looked up the stairs. 'Gabriel,' he said over his houlder.

Fay's stomach turned over. Had he heard her admission of love for him? If he knew, she was lost.

She turned to Sam, her face white.

'Do you think he heard?' she whispered, feeling quite sick.

'I don't know,' he answered honestly. 'I shouldn't think so,' he added, trying to comfort her.

She clutched at his arm. 'When you go back to London will you take me too?' she asked desperately.

Sam touched her white face gently. 'Hey, calm down, love, it's not the end of the world!'

'Will you take me back with you?' she repeated, ignoring him.

'Of course I will, whenever you want to go.'

Fay flung her arms round him thankfully. 'Thank you, Sam! You do understand? I just won't be able to face him again, if he knows.'

Sam held her tightly. 'You really love him,' he said quietly, his voice almost resigned.

'I've loved him from perhaps the first moment I saw him. I don't want to love him, though, not now I know about Danny and Cecilia. He must marry her, and give Danny his name, and I must get away from him.' She was starting to cry, and Sam stroked her hair gently.

'I know, love,' he said softly. 'Don't cry—we can leave whenever you want, Fay.'

'I'll have to speak to Sophie and explain everything, she's been so good to me,' Fay said, wiping her eyes with tense, trembling fingers.

She made her plans as they finished the dinner preparations. It was time she got back to work, maybe she would write to Paul tonight. Now she was physically fit again, hard work would help her forget, she hoped. Making her way upstairs to take a bath before dinner, she heard Danny shrieking with delight in the bathroom. Smiling, she popped her head round the door, to find Sophie, hair dishevelled, covered with water, kneeling at the side of the bath, splashing the little boy, who was retaliating with gusto.

'Sophie, you're soaked!' she exclaimed laughingly.

Her aunt looked up with shining eyes. 'Hello, my dear. Yes, I am, but I'm enjoying myself.'

Fay sat down on a wicker stool, stretching out her legs.

'Cecilia couldn't spare the time, I suppose,' she remarked rather nastily.

Sophie snorted. 'That young woman can't seem to spare any time for Danny. I had it out with her this afternoon, after I got back from the vicarage.'

'So that's where you've been! I seem to have been missing you all day,' Fay exclaimed. 'I wanted to apologise for my behaviour over the last couple of days.'

Sophie shook her head, lifting Danny out of the bath and wrapping him in a huge towel.

'I understand, Fay. Things have been hard for you—Gabriel and Cecilia, Sam turning up. I've sensed that you've wanted to be alone.'

'Dear Sophie, I do love you. I have been depressed and confused, but that's no excuse,' Fay shrugged. 'Tell me about Cecilia.'

Sophie clucked her tongue and began dressing Danny in his pyjamas. He was singing to himself, his eyes full of dreams.

'Well, when I got back, I happened to look in the lounge, and there she was, lying in front of the fire, looking bored to tears, flicking through a magazine as if there wasn't enough work to do around here.' Sophie paused for breath, her face flushed and outraged. 'When she saw me, she gave me one of those stuck-up looks of hers and practically ordered me to make some coffee. So I marched in—I suppose it was quite funny really—and told her that I wasn't a servant, that if she

wanted some coffee, she would have to get off her
backside and make it herself!'

Fay clapped. 'Good for you! I remember the day
she came here, she was ordering me about—in fact,
she actually called me the maid. Anyway, tell me
more.'

Sophie continued, her voice still outraged. 'I asked
her where Danny was, and she said that she thought
he was with Sam and what business was it of mine. I
couldn't help myself, Fay, I lost my temper and told
her that she treated the boy disgracefully, and that it
was his misfortune to have such a mother. I know I
shouldn't have said it, her being so close to Gabe—it's
small wonder to me that he doesn't seem keen to marry
her.'

'He should marry her,' Fay said, her voice quietly
steadfast.

'We don't know the full story, Fay, we can't judge
him.'

'I can. Just looking at Danny should convince him.'
Fay looked at the child with tears in her eyes. He was
cleaning his teeth, his small face screwed up with concentration. He deserved Gabriel's love, attention and
time.

'What did Cecilia say to you?' she asked her aunt.

'That was the funny thing—she just smiled, a
strange smile, and walked out of the room. I felt like
smacking her face! She's a hard, cold woman, Fay.
Would you really condemn Gabriel to a life with her,
if he doesn't love her?'

But Fay would not be moved.

'It's the price he must pay. Would you condemn
Danny to a life without a father?' she asked in a dead
voice.

CHAPTER EIGHT

FAY stepped out of the bath and after drying, pulled on her dressing-gown and made her way back to her bedroom to dress for dinner. She wondered as she dried her hair why Gabriel had never married Cecilia. Fay knew him to be honest and caring; perhaps he had not known of Danny's existence, although from what Fay knew of Cecilia, she could not imagine the other woman keeping quiet for so many years, especially as she obviously wanted Gabriel badly.

Her thoughts were interrupted by Cecilia herself, who walked into her room that very moment, without knocking. Fay turned angrily. 'It's customary to knock before barging into somebody's bedroom,' she said coolly, unable to hide her jealousy and dislike for the beautiful woman who stood before her. Cecilia had everything that Fay wanted—Gabriel and Danny.

Dressed in an apricot chiffon gown that complemented her dark beauty, Cecilia stared at Fay with malicious eyes.

'You'd know all about other people's bedrooms, wouldn't you? What the hell do you think you're up to?' she asked rudely.

Fay stared at her, feeling shocked. Gone was the cold controlled Cecilia, who always smiled so sweetly when she was being snide, and in her place stood an angry uncontrolled woman who was ready to fight for what she wanted.

'I don't know what you're talking about,' Fay answered, still managing to keep her voice cool and steady, because she was telling the truth.

'I think you do,' Cecilia said angrily, her dark eyes insolent as they roamed over Fay, who was still in her underclothes. 'I'm talking about the way you've been throwing yourself at Gabriel.'

Fay coloured, despite her effort not to.

'See—you can't deny it, and you've hardly been discreet. Oh yes, I saw him coming out of this room this morning, and it was fairly obvious what had been going on!'

'Get out of here,' Fay whispered, unable to cope with Cecilia's attack. She wanted to appear cold and as hard as Cecilia, but it was beyond her; she could not match insult for insult. She felt bruised and weary this evening. Cecilia had not moved.

'I'm warning you now, leave him alone. You know the situation, or at least you should do by now,' Cecilia snapped tightly, her eyes hard and spiteful. Fay turned away. Yes, she knew the situation. Cecilia had come here to claim what was hers, and in a strange way, Fay felt sorry for her.

'You have nothing to worry about. I'll be leaving here in the next few days,' she said tiredly.

Cecilia smiled. 'Good. Until then, keep out of his way.'

She strode from the room, leaving Fay alone and rather shaken. This house was becoming unbearable, claustrophobic and intense; the strong emotion that tied all the people together was making them ugly. Fay did not want to be ugly, she just wanted peace to nurse her battered heart.

She dressed for dinner slowly, not wanting to go down, as usual. She did not have to go downstairs, but to stay in her room would be an admission of defeat, and even if she had lost her heart, she still had her pride.

The rich brown crêpe-de-chine dress hugged her

tightly, svelte and sophisticated, and she applied more make-up than usual, trying to mask her uncertainty and her ravaged emotions. She carefully avoided thinking of what Cecilia had said to her; there was plenty of time for that later.

With a final flick to her glossy hair, she went to find Sophie, more determined than ever to make arrangements for leaving. Sophie was in the dining room, setting the dinner table.

'Sophie, can I talk to you?' Fay asked, bringing cutlery from the sideboard and laying it out.

Sophie looked up, hearing the quiet desperation in her niece's voice.

'What is it, child?'

'I'm going back to London with Sam,' Fay blurted out, 'as soon as possible.'

'Must you go?' Sophie asked gently, pausing in her work to watch Fay carefully, with concerned eyes.

Fay bit her lip. 'Yes,' she replied. 'I can't stay here any longer. Oh, Sophie, I can't stand it—Gabriel and Cecilia and Danny, it's driving me mad! Please understand!'

'I do understand, I'm just being selfish. Go whenever you want,' said Sophie, hugging her tightly.

Fay closed her eyes painfully. 'I don't want to leave you, you've been so good to me, so kind, and you know I love you. But loving Gabriel, it's tearing me apart!'

Sophie nodded, understandingly, and Fay continued. 'I'll write, and perhaps I could come up in summer, for a visit. It should have all blown over by then,' she said tearfully, feeling terribly guilty and mean. She was such a coward.

'I understand, Fay, really I do. You mustn't feel guilty—promise me you won't.'

Fay sniffed loudly. 'I promise,' she said huskily.

'Have you and Sam sorted yourselves out?' Sophie

asked casually, changing the subject and carrying on with the table.

'Yes, thank goodness! I think we both realise that marriage would have been a disaster,' Fay smiled. 'We've both grown up too close, I love him as a brother, not a husband.' Her thoughts returned to Gabriel, and her eyes became heavy with pain.

'And Sam knows this?' Sophie had not noticed Fay's sudden misery.

'Yes. He didn't come here to try and make me marry him, as I feared, but just to sort things out. We had a dreadful row before I left. I told him today that I love Gabriel, and I think he's a little jealous, even though there's nothing to be jealous of. I wonder if I'll be jealous when he falls in love? I suppose I will,' she laughed, listening to herself. 'I'm sorry, I'm rambling. Shall we have a drink?'

'Why not? Everything is ready, and I think we deserve a rest.'

They strolled into the lounge, arm in arm, laughing together. Gabriel looked up from his newspaper as they came in and smiled slightly at them. He was alone, which made a change, thought Fay spitefully, as she strolled over to get drinks for herself and Sophie. They sat in front of the fire and she glanced at Gabriel from beneath her lashes, her heart aching with love. He seemed relaxed this evening, his long hard body coiled gracefully in the chair. He lit a cigarette, with deft easy movements, and looked at Fay, his eyes dark and unfathomable.

'I want to talk to you,' he said tonelessly, as if he couldn't care less whether he did or not. 'Will you be free after dinner?'

Fay stared at him suspiciously. 'I don't know, I'm very busy,' she replied coldly, forcing herself not to respond to him.

'Fay's leaving, did you know?' Sophie cut in.

Fay sighed, wishing that her aunt had not spoken. She had been hoping to get away quietly.

Gabriel's face hardened, his hooded eyes glittering. 'Really? When?' he asked casually.

'The day after tomorrow, I think,' Fay replied just as casually, although the words almost choked her. 'Sam's going back then, so I'll go with him.'

'I see,' Gabriel said remotely, drawing deeply on his cigarette.

I doubt it, thought Fay angrily. The news did not seem to matter to him at all. Why had she expected it to be any different? She meant nothing to him, she had known that all along.

'Where's Cecilia?' she asked lightly, her eyes glinting fire at him.

Gabriel shrugged his broad shoulders eloquently. 'I've no idea,' he drawled slowly.

Sophie excused herself and left the room, despite Fay's pleading looks, and they were alone. She got to her feet jerkily. She would not stay in the same room with him alone.

'Running away?' he taunted softly.

'Go to hell!' Fay retorted bitterly, fired by his jibe, turning to leave. He was beside her in a second, his movements sure and lightning-fast, as he grabbed her arm painfully. Fay turned on him, all her anger, frustration and painful love exploding inside her, at the grim smile twisting his suddenly cruel mouth. How could he be so cruel, so casual and uncaring? She was about to walk out of his life for ever and he did not give a damn. It was all too much to bear, loving him as she did, and suddenly losing control, almost unaware of her actions, she delivered a stinging slap across his face, surprising him. She glared at him with feverish green eyes.

'Let me go!'

'Never,' he muttered brutally, twisting his strong fingers into her burnished hair and pulling back her head roughly. 'You've goaded me once too often Fay, and now you'll pay,' he muttered grimly, his silver eyes hungry on her exposed white throat.

She gazed at him fearfully, a shaft of excitement shivering through her. Her lips parted provocatively, unknown to her, and she heard him groan as he took her lips, his mouth hard and insistent. And Fay did not care any more. I love him, she thought achingly, responding mindlessly to his hungry mouth, sliding her hands up over his chest, to the hard, tense muscles of his shoulders. He did not love her, he wanted her, and at that moment she would have accepted anything from him, so weak was she with love and need. His anger was gone, his fingers were gentle in her hair now, and desire shafted through her, as his hands slid to her breasts, his strong, lean fingers caressing her expertly, arousing her. She moaned softly against his mouth, hearing his breathing quickening roughly at her shaking response to his lovemaking. His hands slid to her hips, pulling her closer, moulding her to his hard body, the slender vulnerable softness of her driving him crazy.

The lounge door slamming brought Gabriel's head jerking upwards. Fay felt him stiffen and turned in his arms to see Cecilia standing watching them, her dark eyes deadly with hatred and jealousy. Fay pulled away from Gabriel, feeling the sickness rising in her stomach, dousing the ache of unfulfilled desire, like a cold tide. Cecilia's eyes were boring into her, venomous with rage, and without a word Fay left the room. She could hardly walk, she was shaking so badly, and humiliation blinded her, as she rushed upstairs, nearly knocking Sam over as she collided with him.

'Fay, what's the matter?' he steadied her with strong, gentle hands.

'Sam, will you take me out for dinner tonight? Please? I can't stand to stay here!' She looked at him, half hysterically, her green eyes wide and dull.

Sam nodded his agreement immediately. 'Okay,' he replied, asking no questions.

Fay relaxed thankfully against his young, familiar body, expelling her pent-up breath on a long sigh of pure relief.

'Thank you. Can we go now?'

'Are you all right?' Sam asked, looking down at her with concern.

'Yes—I'm fine. I'll tell you about it later. I'll just let Sophie know that we're going out.'

With renewed strength born of relief, she ran down to the kitchen to tell Sophie, who was a little confused but very understanding.

'Will you come with us?' Fay asked her. But Sophie refused. She wanted to keep an eye on Danny, who she thought might be starting a cold. Fay kissed her quickly and ran up to get her coat.

Gabriel strode from the lounge, as she passed on her way out to the car, where Sam was waiting for her.

'Where are you going?' he asked roughly, his eyes dark and disturbingly savage as they rested on her face.

Fay stared at him, wondering at his foul mood and remembering Cecilia's dark eyes as she had watched them together. She also remembered how Gabriel had stiffened in her arms. Had he felt as guilty as she did now? She had responded so completely, and humiliation rushed over her again, bringing her self-defensive anger with it.

'I'm going out,' she said wearily, wishing that he

would leave her alone. Gabriel shook his head, his face suddenly hard and uncompromising.

'No, you're staying here, I want to talk to you.' His tone was commanding, and to Fay, overbearing. She would not let him order her about!

'Don't try and stop me, Gabriel!' she warned, finding strength from his anger, even managing a cool smile that made her gentle mouth seem almost cruel. 'Sam's waiting for me.'

Gabriel swore savagely. 'Do you think I care?' he muttered dangerously.

'Probably not, you don't seem to care for much,' Fay retorted coldly, able to stand up to him now. 'Are you going to try and stop me?'

He was silent for a moment, his inner struggle obvious. Then, 'Damn you, Fay,' he said tersely, and she knew that he would not stop her, even though he was quite capable of doing so.

Casting him an apprehensive glance, she walked past him, out into the cold night, her heart beating erratically, expecting with every step she took to hear him behind her, stopping her, making her stay with him. Why didn't he stop her? she asked herself remorselessly, wishing in a perverse way that he had. She reached the car and slid in beside Sam.

'Where do you want to go?' he asked smilingly.

'I don't mind. Just drive until we see somewhere,' Fay replied flatly, trying without success to inject some enthusiasm into her voice. 'I'm sorry, Sam, I'm using you. If you prefer to go back, I don't mind,' she said, knowing that he deserved the truth, and disgusted with herself for the way she was treating him.

Sam shrugged. 'I know that you're using me—it doesn't matter,' he replied cheerfully, flashing her a smile, taking his eyes off the road for a moment. 'At least the roads are no worse. Sophie said that she was

expecting to be snowed in this week,' he said, changing
the subject, showing her that he was not hurt. Fay
closed her eyes heavily, tears spilling down her face,
damnable, weak tears. Why did she feel so raw? Sam's
kindness after Gabriel's savagery was affecting her
deeply. Sam pulled off the road, reaching for her,
comforting her as the floodgates burst inside her, and
she sobbed uncontrollably against his jacket, trembling
reaction to the last few hours' events refusing to be
pent up any longer.

'I'll kill him!' Sam muttered viciously, as he
smoothed back her soft hair, wiping away her tears
gently, his face creased with concern.

Finally Fay quietened, her tears spent, leaving her
drained and empty. She gave Sam a weak smile. 'I
must look absolutely dreadful,' she giggled.

'You're beautiful,' Sam replied gently, his eyes telling her the truth of his words.

'I'm not beautiful, but I am hungry,' she said with a
grimace, as she began to repair her make-up.

Sam switched on the engine, laughing. They found
a small inn on the side of the road which looked warm
and friendly, and walked in, hand in hand. It was an
old building with a low, beamed ceiling; they were
shown to a secluded table and Sam ordered drinks. They
sipped them and ordered steak—their taste in food had
always been similar—and salad. Then he eyed Fay over
the table.

'Do you want to talk about it?' he enquired
quietly.

'It was nothing in particular, just another row with
Gabriel, and before that Cecilia came to my room and
warned me away from him—in no uncertain terms,'
she said, looking into his face.

Sam whistled softly. 'She's a hard lady.'

'She was very rude,' Fay remembered angrily. 'It

will serve him right if he does have a life of misery with her.'

'You don't mean that,' Sam said quietly, wishing that she did.

'Maybe not, but one thing's for sure, I won't get involved with them—any more than I have already,' she added hastily, seeing Sam's openly sceptical look.

Their meal arrived at that moment, and they both ate hungrily, hardly speaking until they had finished. Finally Fay sat back replete, a contented smile on her face.

'Have you a cigarette?' she asked.

Sam fished in the pocket of his jacket. 'Some of yours,' he remarked, handing her the half empty packet. 'You left them in the car weeks ago.'

Fay lit one and looked at him, trying to see him through a stranger's eyes. He was a very attractive young man, as cautious glances from various women at other tables testified. His fair hair was cut in a fashionable long style, and his young thin face was full of character, prominent cheekbones and a strong jaw giving him a lean, hungry look. His green eyes slanted, filled with laughter. 'Why are you looking at me like that?' he asked suddenly.

'Like what?'

'In that clinical detached fashion?'

Fay wrinkled up her small nose. 'I was trying to see you as a stranger would see you—you're a very eligible young man.'

Sam shook his head with silent amusement and called for the bill. Fay fumbled in her handbag for her purse and insisted on paying half of the bill, when Sam refused to let her pay all of it.

'Sam,' she muttered with exasperation, 'I asked you to take me out, not the other way round—anyway, I insist.'

They left the restaurant still bickering lightly over the bill. 'Shall we go back?' Sam asked, not pushing her.

'I suppose so.'

'You don't have to, you know,' Sam said as he switched on the engine.

'I do,' Fay replied wearily. 'Running away isn't the answer.' She laid her hand on his arm. 'I'm sorry I couldn't talk about it, but I still feel too raw, too hurt. Do you know what I mean?'

He flashed her a grin and squeezed her hand. 'Forget it. It was good to go out with you—problems and all!' he teased. They arrived back at the house in good time. Sophie met them in the hall.

'Had a good time, you two?' she asked, watching them stamp the snow off their boots.

'It was lovely,' Fay replied. 'Sorry about dinner, Sophie.' She turned to Sam. 'Shall I make some coffee? Will you have a cup, Sophie?'

Sophie and Sam both nodded.

'After a drive like that, a strong cup of coffee would be appreciated,' Sam joked.

Fay glanced towards the lounge and Sophie followed her apprehensive gaze.

'Empty,' she said, answering Fay's unspoken question. 'Miss Tansley has gone to bed and I haven't seen Gabriel for hours. He was in a foul temper at dinner, I suppose you're behind that!' she mock-scolded.

Fay grinned mischievously, as she ran downstairs. She was glad that Gabriel had been angry.

They sat in front of the fire chatting until Fay, unable to stop herself yawning, got to her feet and announced that she was going to bed. The events of the day had worn her out both physically and emotionally and she staggered upstairs hardly able to keep her eyes open, falling asleep immediately.

She was woken in the middle of the night by Gabriel,

shaking her arm gently. She opened her eyes with difficulty, instantly alert, as she saw who was standing over her. The moon was full, lighting the room, flooding his lean face with light and mysterious shadow.

'What's the matter?' she whispered shakily. 'Is it Danny?' She struggled into a sitting position, her forehead creased with worry.

'No, Danny's fine, I've just checked,' Gabriel replied softly, his eyes glittering on her breasts, clearly visible through her filmy nightdress. Fay pulled the sheets up under her chin, swallowing nervously.

'What do you want?' she asked huskily.

'Get up and come for a walk with me,' he commanded softly.

'At this time of night?' Her voice was incredulous.

Gabriel shrugged, his eyes persuasive. 'Why not?'

Fay stared at him as if he were mad, then she smiled.

'Why not indeed?' she laughed gently. She wanted to be with him, and a moonlight walk appealed to her suddenly. 'Wait outside while I dress,' she ordered, softening her command with a smile.

Gabriel leaned over and brushed her mouth briefly with his.

'Put plenty of warm clothes on, it's freezing outside,' he said quietly, as he turned to leave the room.

Fay jumped out of bed as soon as the door closed. She pulled on her jeans, and two thick sweaters, and brushing out her tousled hair was ready. She left the room quietly, her thick woollen socks making no sound on the carpet. Gabriel was waiting just outside her door. His eyes slid over her slowly, appraisingly, and he smiled slightly, his clear eyes warm.

'Come on.' He took her hand and they crept downstairs. Fay found her coat and boots and put them on quickly, trying to suppress the laughter that bubbled in her throat. It reminded her of childhood, creeping around after midnight.

They did not speak until they were outside and walking down the drive. The full moon was high in a clear sky, giving the scenery around them an eerie monochrome brightness. Gabriel slid his arm around Fay's shoulder, and she looked up curiously into his face.

'Do you often walk at this time of night?'

'Only when I can't sleep,' he replied tensely, his veiled eyes scanning the horizon.

'Why can't you sleep?' she persisted gently, still looking into his face.

He glanced down at her briefly.

'You should know,' he said softly.

Fay looked away, her mouth dry. She had not mistaken the violence in his softly spoken voice and it terrified her, even as it thrilled her.

They walked on into the wood, Gabriel's arm still around her shoulder, hard, strong and protective. There was a certain peace between them, almost a bond. It was strange, mused Fay, how one moment they could be at each other's throats, the next in each other's arms, and the next, walking in companionable silence. She would never forget her stormy relationship, brief though it had been, with Gabriel, and she knew with miserable certainty that she would never find another man who obsessed her like he did. Her relationship with Sam was light and uncomplicated, nothing to compare with her deep feelings for the man who walked beside her now.

They had arrived at the top of the hill and Gabriel stopped, turning her to face him.

'I behaved badly this evening,' he said tautly. 'I'm sorry.'

Fay smiled at him. 'It's a difficult situation in the

house at the moment. I suppose we're all under a strain,' she replied, revealing more about her personal feelings than she had intended.

'You don't get on with Cecilia,' he said sardonically, reaching out to touch her cheek with strong, gentle fingers, his eyes difficult to read. Fay shrugged, instinctively shying away from his touch, wondering how to evade the remark. Why should she evade it, though? She was leaving in a day or so.

'No,' she answered flatly. 'I'm sorry.'

Gabriel smiled grimly, noticing her withdrawal from him.

'And Danny?' he asked, his voice careful and intense.

'He's lovely,' Fay replied immediately, her face gentle with love.

'You care for him?' He watched her intently as he asked.

'Of course I do—anybody would care for him.' Except Cecilia, his own mother, she thought silently.

Gabriel took her arm and they continued walking.

'Were you a happy child, Fay?' he asked.

'Yes, I was happy, and even though I'm an only child, I was never lonely because there was Sam and the rest of his family. What about you?' She felt reluctant to talk about herself, not wanting him to know too much about her; it was too late.

Gabriel's grey eyes became reminiscent. 'Alex and I were brought up in Sicily by an uncle, after our parents were killed. We grew up very close—our uncle never really cared for us, we were an unwanted responsibility for him. We had a good life, don't misunderstand, warm and sunny and wild, that's how I remember it,' he said, smiling at her. 'God, we were reckless, life was too easy for us, I guess, and Alex. . . .' He sighed tiredly. 'Alex died as he lived.'

Fay reached up and touched his firm mouth. 'Gabriel, I'm sorry, I didn't mean to make you think of. . . ,' Her voice trailed off, uncertain of what she wanted to say to him, her eyes green pools of sadness.

'You're so gentle, Fay,' he said harshly, as if her gentleness hurt him. He captured her hand and pressed his lips to her sensitive palm, his eyes holding hers. The touch of his mouth shivered through her body, awakening her nerve-ends with shock and desire. She pulled her hand away from him, trying to ignore the mockery in his silver eyes as she did so.

Her thoughts were filled with him and his brother as children, running wild under hot foreign skies, Gabriel older, protective, looking out for his brother always. Strangely her thoughts hurt her, twisting her heart, but she needed to know more, and turned to him.

'Tell me about your life,' she begged.

He stared down at her with clear, curious eyes, wondering at her question and her pleading tone, then he shrugged carelessly.

'I was brought up in Sicily, as I've said. I came to England for school, and university, after which I took various jobs, and travelled—the usual kind of thing. I started to write and here I am.' It was a very brief précis. He had told her nothing, as if he too were reluctant to build anything more between them.

'How old were you when your parents died?' she asked quietly, not giving up.

'Seven,' he replied briefly. Then, 'We were sent to Sicily almost immediately, it was a confusing time— for me anyway. Alex was only a baby. Let's walk.'

He placed his arm around her shoulder again, hugging her close, and they walked. Gradually, the stiff restraint between them dissolved and, urging him to talk about himself again, Fay built up a picture of his life.

As a sad aggressive child, confused by the sudden loss of his parents, and his new life abroad, he had been wild and rebellious, fiercely protective of his younger brother, the only person he loved, having lost the rest of his family. Brought up by an uncle who did not care for them, left to roam free in the wild alien countryside of Sicily. Fighting the hitherto unknown discipline of an English school—all these things had stamped his character, made him strong and resistant. He had travelled widely, and had worked at many jobs, finally choosing writing as a career, at which he excelled. His had been a strange and conflict-filled life, so different from Fay's. Her life had been neat and ordinary. Her fairly secure family and uneventful schooldays all made it difficult to comprehend Gabriel's life, a life that had made him hard and forceful, smooth and complex.

Fay wondered about the women he had known. She had seen pictures in the newspapers, articles linking his name with various beautiful and famous women. He was experienced, that was obvious, and the newspapers gave the impression of a rich, easy life, liberally dotted with stormy, casual affairs. Knowing Gabriel as she did now, she found it hard to believe. He cared for people, and she knew for certain that he would not discard them so easily, so casually. But she did not ask him about the women; she did not want to know.

As soon as she got back to London, she resolved to go to the library and borrow all his books. She found herself longing to read them, although for some reason she could not bring herself to disclose this fact to him.

Looking up, she discovered that they had walked a wide circle, and were back in the woods in front of the house. Gabriel was silent, preoccupied, his arm still protectively about her.

'What did you want to talk to me about?' she asked casually.

'It doesn't matter,' he answered brusquely, making it clear that he would not tell her. He seemed angry, his face hard and austere.

'Please yourself,' Fay said lightly, hiding her hurt feelings.

He flashed her a dark glance. 'When do you leave?' he asked stiffly, stopping suddenly, and she found her back against the wide trunk of a tree, Gabriel's arms on either side of her, trapping her.

'The day after tomorrow,' she replied, licking her lips nervously, staring up into his face as if hypnotised.

'Back to the safe, comfortable life. Is that what you want, Fay?' he asked savagely, his face only inches from her own, a shadowed mask, his glittering eyes hungry as they rested on her mouth.

'It's what I want,' she answered defiantly, lying to him. He must never know the truth.

'You want me,' he murmured, his silver eyes sliding to the hammering pulse in her white throat, with dark triumph.

Fay shifted uneasily, achingly aware that she could not get away from him.

'Your conceit never fails to amaze me,' she managed coldly.

Gabriel laughed out loud, as his hands closed on her waist, pulling her against him violently. She felt the hard strength of his legs against her own, with a shock of sensual awareness.

'Don't deceive yourself, my love. You want me,' he repeated, 'almost as much as I want you. It's always been this way between us, you know that.' His warm breath fanned her cheek as he spoke.

'No!' Fay moaned softly, denying his words, twisting futilely in his strong arms, fighting herself and the weak languor that his nearness induced.

'Yes, Fay, admit it,' he said thickly as he lowered his dark head. She felt the violent passion in him as their mouths touched and her love was too strong to deny him. Her lips parted of their own volition, beneath his fierce demanding mouth, and even through her coat she could feel the heavy pounding of his racing heart. Their mouths moved endlessly together, Fay's soft and yielding, Gabriel's hard and hungry, fusing exploringly. There was nothing in the world but his mouth and his hands, sliding gently through her hair.

Dizzily Fay reached up to steady herself, clutching at his broad shoulders. She heard him groan against her lips, his hands trembling at her throat as they slid beneath her sweater, to find the soft bare skin of her shoulders, caressing her sweetly, achingly, until she was mindless, boneless. She whispered his name over and over as his mouth moved over her face, covering it with hungry, tender kisses. Reluctantly, he lifted his proud head, his grey eyes burning with desire.

'Tell me now,' he groaned, breathing hard. 'Tell me now that you don't want me.'

Fay stared at him with wide, bitter eyes, as the impact of his words sank in. Yes, she wanted him, more than anything in the world, she was desperate for him, but she would never admit it to him. Never. Gathering all her strength, she pulled herself from the strong circle of his arms, and began to run towards the house as quickly as she could. Deep inside herself, she was screaming. She did not look back until she reached the front door. He had not moved. He stood on the hill watching her, his body tall and still with nameless defeat. She had lied again. . . .

*

She woke very late the next morning from a deep, dreamless and exhausted sleep that had not come until dawn. She had lain in bed restlessly, after the walk, waiting for Gabriel to come in. He did not come in, and she cursed him savagely even as she longed for him to come to her bed and love her, to ease the pain inside her. After showering and dressing she went downstairs in search of some strong black coffee, but as she approached the lounge on her way to the kitchen, Cecilia's cool voice, pleading in her tone, wafted out of the half-open door.

'He's your responsibility, Gabriel,' she was saying desperately.

'You think I don't know that?' Gabriel's voice was hard and angry. 'He is my responsibility, and I want him.'

Fay leaned against the wall, feeling sick, a searing pain ripping at her insides. At last Gabriel had admitted that Danny was his son, that he wanted him, and Fay thought her heart would break. He was lost for ever to her, and this fact finally hit her, even though she had known ever since Cecilia and Danny had arrived here. Despite herself, she could not help listening to the ensuing conversation.

'I'm glad you're ready to face up to it,' Cecilia said coldly. 'We could all live here.' Her voice was soft and pleading and Fay imagined her staring into his grey eyes, touching his arm helplessly.

'No, Cecilia.' Gabriel was unyielding, his voice still hard, cold and brutal. There was silence for a moment.

'Why not, Gabriel? It's your house. We'd be happy, I promise you.' Cecilia was beginning to sound tearful.

Fay stood rooted to the spot, guiltily aware that she should not be listening to this private, damning conversation, but unable to move a muscle.

'It's Sophie's house,' Gabriel muttered harshly.

'You own it,' Cecilia accused, her voice trembling.

'I've told you, the answer is no!' His savagery frightened Fay, and she felt compassion for Cecilia, who was sobbing noisily.

Suddenly Gabriel was at the door, striding from the room, his eyes dangerous, his mouth tight and violent. Fay shrivelled up inside, and shrank against the wall, as his eyes flicked over her disdainfully.

'Eavesdropping?' he enquired unpleasantly, not waiting for her answer, as he strode away, his powerful body taut with anger. Fay watched him go fearfully, her legs like jelly.

Cecilia was still sobbing and Fay forced herself to move away from the door and into the dining room. She sat down at the table and buried her face in her hands. She groaned out loud, unable to believe Gabriel's cruelty, his heartlessness in rejecting the mother of his child so brutally.

Then she remembered something that hit her like a bomb. Gabriel owned this house. She repeated it to herself slowly. Was it true? If he did own the house, then Sophie had no security here.

Praying with all her heart that it was a mistake, Fay got shakily to her feet and ran like the wind downstairs.

'Sophie, tell me honestly—does Gabriel own this house?' She stared at her aunt with wild, hysterical eyes.

Sophie flushed, lowering her eyes. 'Yes, he owns it, but. . . .'

Fay turned on her heel and ran from the room, ignoring her aunt, who was calling to her to come back.

She was mad with fury as she rushed upstairs to

Gabriel's flat. She would not let him get away with this. Without bothering to knock, she flung open his door and stormed inside. He was standing by the window, his broad shoulders hunched and tense. Fay stood behind him, breathing fast, watching him with hatred, as he slowly turned to face her, his grey eyes ice-cold.

'Get out!' he said angrily, dismissing her cruelly.

Fay stared at him. He had destroyed her life, and probably Sophie's too, but she knew at that moment that it was her deep, aching love that was making her so furious. He did not love her—it was a defeating admission, and she wanted to hurt him, as he had hurt her.

'I won't!' she snapped at him. 'Somebody has to stand up to you, and somebody has to stand up for Sophie.'

'What the hell are you talking about?' he asked grimly.

'You swine!' Fay choked, withering beneath his icy, contemptuous gaze. 'You know damn well what I'm talking about. You stole Sophie's house, and I won't let you get away with it!'

A tight smile twisted Gabriel's cruel mouth but did not reach his eyes.

'You shouldn't listen in on other people's conversations,' he drawled coldly. 'But as you seem to make a habit of it—yes, I own this house and there's not a thing you can do about it, so get out.' He turned away, finished with her, his boredom obvious.

Without thinking, taking notice only of the blind anger inside herself and the pain he had inflicted on her, Fay began raining blows on his back with all her strength, her small fists pounding and clawing at his broad shoulders.

Gabriel spun round and grabbed her slender wrists,

pulling them down easily and twisting them painfully behind her back, his strong fingers crushing her fragile bones. Fay had never seen him so angry and she became still immediately, biting her lower lip until she tasted blood, determined not to cry out with pain.

'You violent little bitch!' he gritted through clenched teeth, and shook her roughly, making her wince with agony.

She stared defiantly into his lean twisted face. 'I hate you,' she said slowly, enunciating every word clearly. 'What are you going to do? Break my arms?'

'I'd like to kill you,' Gabriel muttered softly, his silver eyes savage.

'I don't care!' Fay cried recklessly, her anger suddenly gone, to be replaced with cold, heavy misery. She wished she had not come up here. It had done no good; he still owned the house, and as he had said, there was nothing in the world she could do about it.

Still staring down at her, Gabriel suddenly released her, so abruptly that she nearly fell over.

'Get out of here, Fay,' he repeated coldly.

'You're a cheat, and a cruel, horrible person! You don't care about anybody but yourself. This is Sophie's house, and you've taken it from her, you've tricked her just as you've tricked Cecilia and Danny. I'll never forgive you!'

Gabriel's fists clenched at his sides, his body perfectly still, a dull red flush along his hard cheekbones, as she spoke to him, her voice as dead as her green eyes. Fay turned on her heel and left the room, tears coursing down her cheeks. She had done what she set out to do when she had come up here, driven by anger, and a need for revenge. She had hurt him, although the knowledge gave her no pleasure, as she stumbled into her bedroom. She had to leave today. It was over.

CHAPTER NINE

THEY drove to a small restaurant well known to them both, in the West End of London, almost in silence. Although Fay had resolved not to spoil Sam's meal by being miserable, there was little to say, and she felt both physically and mentally exhausted. She was home again, and all the urgency of her flight from Yorkshire that morning was gone, leaving her feeling like an empty shell.

She had sat in Sam's car after saying goodbye to Sophie and Danny, feeling as if she wanted to die as he switched on the engine, and then they had driven off, with Sophie waving from the front door, and Fay waving back with the nagging suspicion that she had left something behind, knowing that her life was in ruins. She had known that Sophie wanted to speak with her before she left, but she had put it off, unable to cope with anything more. She had left Danny reluctantly; it was like leaving her own child, it hurt so much, and she had realised just how much she had come to love him. She had not seen Gabriel or Cecilia.

The journey had been a nightmare. As the car had turned on to the motorway, it had seemed as if the last bonds were cut and she was free. The trouble was that Fay did not want her freedom, had forgotten what to do with it. They had stopped once at a motorway café, where Sam had eaten a big meal, and Fay had fiddled endlessly with her black coffee until it was time to get back into the car. She had bought some cigarettes and had smoked almost continually, even though the smoke

in her empty stomach had made her feel sick, until
they reached the outskirts of London. It was a different
world, grim, noisy and wet with rain, when only a few
hours before they had been surrounded by fresh air,
peace and thick white snow.

Sam had driven straight to her flat, his face dark
with concern. Darkness was falling rapidly and he had
insisted on coming into the flat with her to check that
everything was in order. Fay had pushed open the
green front door with mixed feelings—relief and pain.
She picked up the pile of letters that had accumulated
during her absence and switched on the lights. Sam
came in behind her with her suitcases and put them
down in the hall. The flat smelled stale, Fay thought
distastefully, wrinkling up her nose. She would have
to clean it out; at least it would give her something to
do.

'I wouldn't say no, if you insisted I stayed for coffee,'
Sam grinned endearingly. Fay smiled, realising how
she had been ignoring him.

'I'll put the kettle on. Perhaps you could switch on
the fire, it's quite chilly in here.' Pulling off her coat,
she went into the kitchen. 'There's no milk—Sam, be
an angel and pop next door, ask Angie if I can borrow
half a bottle until tomorrow,' she shouted over her
shoulder. She heard the front door bang as Sam left.

Fay stared round the tiny kitchen, her eyes resting
on the neat yellow units. The whole place seemed
curiously untouched, familiar, almost as if there was
nowhere else in the world, and all the things that had
happened over the past few weeks had been a dream,
from which she had now woken.

Shrugging off these maudlin thoughts, she filled the
kettle with water and switched it on. She felt faint with
hunger even though she did not feel as if she could
face any food. Sam would be hungry, though, and the

least she could do was to cook him some dinner. She looked through the cupboards with increasing dismay. Apart from some crackers and a piece of cheese, there was absolutely no food in the flat.

Sam came back with the milk, his thin face flushed. Fay smiled at him lovingly, seeing his embarrassment.

'Has Angie been trying her fatal charm on you?' she teased.

Sam blushed brighter. 'I'm taking her out to dinner next Friday,' he admitted almost shyly.

'That's great!' Fay answered, meaning it. She made coffee for them both. 'I wanted to make something to eat, but there's no food.'

Sam looked in all the cupboards and the fridge. 'That settles it, then,' he said brightly. 'I'm taking you out for dinner.'

'You don't have to—really! I'm not very hungry,' Fay protested.

Sam ignored her. 'We'll go as soon as we've had our coffee,' he said firmly, not willing to argue.

Fay sighed, knowing that she was beaten. They sat by the fire and she flicked idly through her mail, not bothering to open any of it. Looking up, she found Sam watching her and tried to smile.

'I want to thank you Sam, for. . . .' she began.

He jumped to his feet, and pulled Fay to hers. 'Thank me after dinner,' he laughed. 'I'm starving!'

She could not help laughing with him, at this heartfelt declaration.

'Right, I'll just go and fix my face.' She went to the bedroom and exchanged her boots for slender-heeled shoes, then brushed out her hair vigorously, deciding not to change. She washed her face, then applied foundation and blusher in an effort to hide the pallor of her face. She stroked green shadow on to her eyelids and darkened her lashes with mascara. Lipstick, carefully applied, was the final touch, and although not satisfied with her appearance, she was ready.

She managed nearly all of her ham omelette and salad, by washing it down with plenty of wine. Sam watched her drinking more than usual in frowning silence.

Fay thanked him for bringing her back from York-shire at such short notice, with her heart in her eyes as they sat outside her flat, later. She refused to let him come in; the strain of appearing bright and carefree had taken its toll and she feared she would burst into tears as soon as she got inside. Sam accepted it, kissing her gently, and promised to ring her the following day, as she slid out of the car.

Then at last she was alone, and despite Sam's kind-ness, it was a relief. Bolting the front door, she went to sit in front of the fire. And although she fought it, her thoughts turned to Gabriel. His face, a dark mask of anger, insinuated itself into her mind, making her remember the urgent, passion-filled moments she had spent in his arms. The remembered touch of his warm mouth and his strong hands taunted her, until she cried out and sank to her knees, sobbing violently, tears that took all her strength.

She went to bed an hour later, her movements mech-anical as she washed and undressed. She fell asleep al-most immediately, utterly exhausted, and did not wake up until well after noon the next day, when she was jerked back to consciousness by the telephone ringing persistently by her bedside. She reached for it sleepily, to find that it was Sam, checking that she was all right, worrying about her as always. Reassuring him briefly, she hung up and lay back in bed, misery and depression washing over her as she remembered where she was and what had happened. Her dreams came back to her vividly, all of Gabriel, tense with anger, tender with passion, and she did not want to get up. She wanted to go back to those dreams, to sleep for ever.

At last she dragged herself out of bed, feeling tired and weepy. She would have to make some sort of effort, she supposed, to get her life back together again. She would start today. She had lost Gabriel, she would love him for ever, and her love and her memories would make her strong—she hoped.

She showered and dressed in old jeans and a Fair Isle sweater, then listed all the things she had to do that day. She was hurting inside, but she was a fighter; nobody would ever know that her heart was broken and perhaps in the end she would believe it herself. She would fill every moment of her day, not leave herself any time to think of Gabriel, and she would find him at night in her dreams. Would that be enough? It would have to be.

Shopping came first, and armed with a list and a basket she grabbed her coat, and left the flat, stopping to chat to Angie on her way out. She bought fruit and vegetables first, then all the other things on her list before making her way to the library, fighting her impulse to do so all the way. There were three of Gabriel's books on the shelves. She put them into her basket on the way out, with trembling hands, as if they were part of him that she was touching.

She walked slowly back to her flat, squashing the impatience inside her, stopping to chat to various people she met. Once at home she stored away her provisions carefully and placed Gabriel's books gently on the table. She picked one up and held it in her hands for long moments. The knowledge that he had written it brought him closer to her. It was filled with his words, his thoughts and his imagination. She did not feel strong enough to read it just yet, but just to have it near her was enough.

Sam had advised her to try and forget him, to start again, find a new lover, but as she held Gabriel's book, she realised that she did not want to forget him, she wanted to remember everything, to nurture her memories of time spent with him, however unhealthy that would seem to Sam.

She opened the book and stared at the small and awful photograph on the dust jacket, with a pounding heart. His face stared back at her, hard and forceful, his clear eyes carefully blank, his mouth relaxed and quite gentle. It was a shock to her and she could feel the tears closing her throat. She put the book down carefully again and lit a cigarette with shaking hands, drawing on it deeply to steady her nerves, repeating his name over and over again in her mind.

Later that afternoon she telephoned her parents, who were pleased and surprised to hear from her and invited her over for dinner that evening, and Paul, her boss, who sounded ecstatic when she told him that she would be back at work the following Monday. He invited her out to dinner that evening and when she refused, explaining her prior commitment, he asked her for the following evening, which was Sunday. Fay accepted readily, laughing at his enthusiasm as he told her about his current film. He made no pretence about how pleased he would be to have her back, and she felt needed again. She was very fond of Paul, he was kind, considerate and extremely talented, and it was a pleasure to work for him.

The evening spent with her parents was largely taken up with questions about her broken engagement. Both her parents were shocked by her actions, and did not hide it. It had never occurred to them that she would not marry Sam. Fay explained the situation to them, it was easy to talk about Sam, and she felt profoundly thankful that they knew nothing of Gabriel.

Sunday was spent cleaning out her flat thoroughly. It was hard, tiring work, but it gave her no time to think, which was a blessing, and not finishing until late, she had to rush to get ready for her dinner date with Paul.

She strolled into the restaurant where they had agreed to meet only ten minutes late. Paul was waiting for her, twirling a glass in his hand with obvious impatience—he hated people to be late. Fay gave him a warm smile as she approached the table. His shrewd blue eyes slid over her questioningly, not fooled for a second by the make-up she had used to try and hide the agonising strain of the past few days. His calculating gaze also took in the fact that she had lost weight, even though the expensively-cut wool dress she was wearing hid the fact admirably.

'You're late,' he said, his voice devoid of expression.

'Yes, I'm sorry.' Fay was used to his blunt manner, knowing that excuses were wasted on him.

'Drink?'

'A glass of wine would be nice,' she answered vaguely, somehow reassured by the fact that he had not changed. It was strangely comforting to know that she was the only one who had changed. 'And stop looking at me so intently!' she added sternly.

Paul raised his shaggy eyebrows mockingly. 'I'm curious,' he said innocently.

'I'm not going to tell you anything,' Fay replied with a smile.

'No?'

'No, so you might as well give up now.'

Paul shrugged carelessly and they ordered their meal. Not feeling at all hungry, Fay chose soup, which was at least easy to get down her easily-blocked throat, and a salad. Her appetite seemed to have disappeared since she had left Yorkshire and she was losing more weight, but there was nothing she could do about it. Urging Paul to talk about his present film—anything to steer the conversation away from herself—she watched him carefully as she automatically spooned up her soup, not tasting it at all. It was good to see him again, she thought as her eyes slipped over him, taking in his cropped dark hair and thin intelligent face. They knew each other well and got on easily. When she had first met him a few years before, she had often been shocked by his bluntness, and he had made it clear that while he found her 'delightfully attractive', he had no intention of letting any emotional or sexual relationship spring up between them to affect their work. This bald statement had decided Fay to take the job he had offered. She had not trusted him at first, but as time had passed it became obvious that he had been telling the truth, obvious in fact that he hardly saw her as a woman at all. They had developed a superb working relationship and a slow friendship had built up between them, as Fay had gradually relaxed her mistrust.

'You're not listening,' Paul suddenly accused, bringing her out of her thoughtful reverie.

'No,' she agreed honestly. There was no point in arguing with him, he always chose his words carefully, and he was usually right.

'I suppose it's excusable as we're not working,' he said drily, staring at her. 'You don't look much better for your holiday.'

'Stop fishing,' said Fay, unable to suppress a smile at his lack of tact.

'Okay, but if you do want to pour your heart out, I expect I could just about bear to listen, offer the proverbial shoulder,' he replied extravagantly. Fay recognised his sincerity.

'Thanks, I appreciate it, and I'll let you know if I need your shoulder,' she promised with a smile.

Paul hailed a taxi as they left the restaurant some time later, and they both got in. He never drove, considering it a waste of time, when somebody could do it for him. He liked to think when he was travelling, and not have to concentrate on the road. He dropped her off at her flat.

'Thanks for the dinner,' she said politely, as she slid from the taxi.

'Be early tomorrow,' he replied, ignoring her thanks, as the taxi drove off.

She went to bed immediately, knowing that when Paul said be early, he meant it, and he allowed nothing to interfere with his work. Her thoughts turned to Gabriel as she lay in bed unable to sleep, and a longing to see him, to touch him, made her tremble violently as her tears came, releasing all the tense, desperate emotion she had managed all day to keep pent up, and finally she escaped into her dreams.

She went back to work the next day, glad to be busy again. It was not difficult to submerge herself, because typically, Paul had not employed anybody to replace her while she had been away, and there was a mountainous backlog of work to be dealt with.

'Good grief, Paul!' she groaned when she saw her desk. 'It looks as though a bomb's hit it ... there's letters here dated two months ago. Why didn't you get a temp?'

He looked up absently from his work, smiling slightly at her outraged face. 'Nobody knows the work like you do—it would have taken me all this time to train a temp, and besides, I dealt with all the really urgent business myself.'

Fay sighed loudly as she sat down, hardly able to believe that such an intelligent man could be so impractical, and started sifting through the enormous piles of papers, documents and correspondence in front of her. Paul appeared at her side five minutes later with a cup of coffee and a conciliatory smile. He perched himself on the side of her desk.

'I suppose I should have got somebody in,' he said by way of an apology, as if he had suddenly realised just how much work there was to do. 'Tell me about your holiday.'

'No,' Fay replied defensively, determined not to tell him about Gabriel.

Paul's light blue eyes flicked over her suddenly flushed face with interest. 'A man?' he asked shrewdly.

'Mind your own business,' she answered mildly. 'And even if you have no work to do, as you can see, I have plenty.'

Paul laughed. 'You'll tell me in the end,' he asserted infuriatingly, ignoring her sarcasm.

He left soon afterwards for a meeting with his director, and Fay worked steadily all day, taking only a quick break for coffee at lunchtime, until she had cleared her desk. Then, feeling thoroughly worn out, she went home early, one of the advantages of her job being that she never worked fixed hours. She closed the front door of her flat with a feeling of extreme relief, and picked up her mail. There was a bill and a letter from Sophie, and Fay's hand shook alarmingly as she recognised the handwriting. She had not been expecting to hear from her aunt so soon and her heart began to hammer as she tore open the envelope. Please let there be some news of Gabriel, she prayed as she pulled the letter out. She walked into the lounge feeling pale and weak-kneed, and sitting down in front of the fire, began to read.

'My dear Fay,' her aunt began, in her small neat handwriting, 'I didn't get a chance to talk to you before you left, and I feel that there's something you must know about Gabriel. I could see how desperately upset you were, so I decided to leave it until I could write to you. I couldn't help hearing you both shouting on Friday, you were arguing about the house, and I'm going to explain about it.

'When I told you about Gabriel renting the flat, I left out the fact that I was desperate to take in a lodger. I haven't told anybody this, not even your mother, but after Arthur died, I found out that he had been a compulsive gambler—I'd had no idea while he was alive, not even a hint.' Fay tore her gaze from the letter, and stared into the fire with wide troubled eyes. It must have been very difficult for Sophie to write all this down, and she felt like crying. Her aunt must have suffered so very much, and she had told nobody. She lowered her head and read on.

'When the will was sorted out, and we went through all his papers, I found that he'd mortgaged the house and run up thousands of pounds in gambling debts. I found that I was literally in debt for thousands, with not a penny to pay them off. I tried to manage and the idea of a lodger in the flat seemed a good one, and after Gabriel came here, I did manage for a couple of months, until a particularly large bill came up for payment and I realised that the only way out was to sell the house.

'As you can imagine, dear Fay, the thought of doing so was unbearable, I love this house, it holds all my memories. Gabe found me weeping one morning in the kitchen—I was so low, I just blurted out the whole story. He offered to give me the money, that's the sort of man he is, money is not particularly important to him. I couldn't accept, of course, so he offered a loan. That too was out of the question, I had no way of paying him back. It was my suggestion that he buy the house—he wanted a house, and I thought if he owned this one, I could visit sometimes, and I wouldn't be losing it to a stranger. I persuaded him, Fay, and that's important for you to know. It was never like you think, he gave me a high price, more than the house is worth, and I paid off all Arthur's debts—it was like coming out of a long dark tunnel—I couldn't thank him enough.

'I told him that I'd leave as soon as possible, but he wouldn't let me. He made up some story that he didn't want to live here permanently, said he just wanted the house as an investment, for tax purposes, or some such nonsense, and that I'd have to stay to look after the place. I hope you understand, Fay, he hasn't cheated me, he's given more than he ever had to, more than I ever expected in my wildest dreams. And that's why I've written to you, because he doesn't deserve your thinking of him so badly. He's a remarkable man. I realise that I should have told you before you left, but I was feeling too upset, and to be quite honest too cowardly. . . .'

Fay let the letter drop from her numb fingers, not bothering to read any more, staring blindly into space, her mind whirling, unaware of the warm tears washing down her face. She had been terribly wrong about Gabriel, and it was too late to apologise, although she knew that any words she could have said to him would not be enough. She had hurt him, the damage was done, he would not forgive her easily. She groaned, a cold mist of horror settling on her mind, as she remembered what she had said to him, and then in a blinding flash of hope, she realised that if she had been wrong about the house, then maybe she had been wrong about Danny and Cecilia. But no, Cecilia had more than hinted that Gabriel belonged to her, and Danny's likeness to Gabriel could not be easily dismissed. It did not matter any more; he was lost to her, it was more than likely that she would never see him again.

Fay lit a cigarette, and thought about her strong, unswerving love for him. She had never known love until she met Gabriel. She had been drawn to him, very much against her will, from the moment she had first set eyes on him, on that lonely station. She remembered, with crystal clarity, looking at him, being held by his graceful movement, by his lean shadowed face, and that was when she had begun to fight, automatically, instinctively knowing that he, of all the men she had ever met, could break the ring of ice that she had carefully constructed around her heart. And he had done so with such ease, right from the beginning, forcing her to admit that she desired him, making her hate and mistrust him, even as she began to love him, for trying to put her in the same position that her mother had been in so many years before.

She had been very aware of the dangers of feeling so deeply for a man, and she had fought herself as viciously as she had fought him—all to no avail. She had fallen deeply in love with him, and as she got to know him better, it became obvious that he had no intention of hurting her; he was gentle and honest and strong, he had never deceived her. Nonetheless, right up to that last awful day at Lambrigg House, she had been more than ready to believe the worst of him, had pounced on any opportunity to see him as an unfeeling monster in an effort to kill the desperate, hopeless love that she feared could destroy her, as it had destroyed her mother.

Did she see things differently now? She hoped so, it seemed that falling in love had taught her something. It had freed her from all the years of inhibition, when she had blamed all men for what had happened to one woman. She was glad that she loved Gabriel, even though she had lost him. Her only regret was that they had not become lovers. Even a brief affair, with all the heartbreaking consequences, might have been worth it, just to have known him, to have known the ecstasy she was sure he could have given her, and would have given her more to cherish on miserable lonely evenings such as this.

Fay covered her face with her hands, amazed at her own thoughts. She might love him, but he did not love her, and there was still Danny and Cecilia. His dark, beautiful face flashed before her closed eyes, accusing her bitterly, and she gave herself up to her tears again.

Sam met her from work the next day, strolling into the tiny office just before five and smiling at her brightly.

'What time do you finish?' he asked, kissing her cheek lightly.

'Now,' she answered, returning his smile. 'Why?'

'Will you have dinner with me?'

'Mm, yes. If you'll just give me five minutes to tidy up here, I'll be with you,' Fay replied, her attention still on her work.

'Still working you to death, is he?' Sam asked, staring out of the window, across the murky river.

'You know Paul,' Fay replied wryly, deftly gathering together contracts and letters for Paul to sign, and placing them on his cluttered desk.

Sam's eyes slid over her worriedly as she brushed her shiny, burnished hair, taking in her unusually slender figure and the dark, bruised circles beneath her eyes, but he said nothing. He was aware of just how difficult it was for her to try and carry on, day after day, pretending to the world that there was nothing wrong with her.

But Fay caught his worried glance. 'Sam, I hope you're not taking me out because you feel sorry for me. If you are, there's really no need. . . .'

'I want to take you out, so be quiet and get ready,' he said, raising his eyes dramatically.

When they were seated at their table sipping pre-dinner drinks, Sam took her hand. 'How are you?' he asked gently.

Fay looked into his serious, concerned face, and managed a smile, she was really getting rather good at smiling when she really felt like bursting into tears. 'I'm coping, just about,' she replied honestly. 'And Paul with his endless, endless work is helping. Don't worry about me, Sam.'

'I can't help it, you know that. I've worried about you for years,' he joked. 'I saw Angie yesterday, by the way,' he added casually, although Fay could tell by his eyes that he was not feeling casual.

'I thought you'd arranged to see her this Friday?'

'We met by accident, in Oxford Street. We went for a drink.' He was obviously a little embarrassed, his face slightly flushed.

Fay smiled at him, feeling almost maternal. 'You like her a lot,' she said gently.

Sam nodded, still embarrassed. 'She reminds me of you a little, and she's very pretty. We get on like a house on fire—the first time we met, I don't know, something seemed to spark between us, do you understand?'

Fay nodded miserably. She understood only too well, it had happened with Gabriel and herself.

She picked at her meal when it arrived, unable to manage more than a few choking mouthfuls, and was angry with herself. If she did not get a good meal soon, she would make herself ill.

Sam drove her back to her flat and she asked him in

for coffee. When she carried the tray into the lounge, she found him flicking through one of Gabriel's books, with sad eyes.

'I got them from the library,' Fay explained haltingly. 'They seem to bring him closer to me, somehow.' To her horror, she burst into tears, and with a groan Sam took her into his arms and comforted her. She felt stupid and embarrassed, and he left soon after, understanding that she felt awkward.

As a couple of weeks passed, her life fell back into the old pattern that was familiar and so safe. The memory of her time spent at Lambrigg House gradually faded and became less real, only her deep love for Gabriel remained strong and crystal clear. And as the time passed she became a little stronger, never confiding in anybody but Sam about her misery. It was easy to put up a front, a strong wall around her aching heart, and at least she had got rid of the ice that had once surrounded her. All these things helped her to slowly recover.

Letters from Sophie came regularly, mentioning Gabriel briefly, now and again. They also mentioned Danny, although tantalisingly; Sophie never clarified the situation. For all Fay knew Gabriel could have married Cecilia by now, and although she always wrote back to Sophie asking to know what was going on, her aunt never answered these questions and remained infuriatingly vague.

Fay still cried at nights. She would never get over Gabriel.

CHAPTER TEN

A MONTH after her return to London, Fay came home late from work one evening to find a low, powerful bottle-green sports car parked outside her flat. She stared at it curiously—she knew nobody with a car like that. Perhaps it was somebody visiting Angie; Sam would not be too pleased if it was, she thought wryly. Sam and Angie had been seeing each other fairly regularly since the evening Sam had borrowed the milk from her. They got on very well and Fay was sure that Sam was already a little in love.

Shrugging, she opened her front door and dropped her briefcase as soon as the door was shut. It had been a particularly tiring day, her muscles were aching and she decided to take a hot relaxing bath before preparing her solitary dinner. She strolled into the bedroom, idly sifting through her mail, her mind still on work, and a location problem that Paul and herself had been wrestling with for days, and began to undress. One of the best things about her job, she had decided, was the fact that it was so all-consuming, taking her mind off her own problems. Paul had boundless energy and a remarkably creative mind, but like many people of this type he was totally impractical. Detail bored him, so everything practical was dealt with by Fay, which suited them both admirably, leaving them to work together in perfect harmony.

Musing happily on this, Fay slipped on a silk wrap, yellow, and scattered with pale embroidered flowers, and began to run her bath. She was just reaching for some wildly expensive perfumed bath crystals, having decided to be extravagant, when the door bell rang loudly.

Sighing irritably, she wandered out into the hall, hoping that it wasn't Paul with more problems, and opened the door.

It was not Paul who stood outside, but Gabriel. Fay's heart began to race as she stared at him, taking in his long dark untidy hair—he needed a hair-cut, she thought inconsequentially—and the tired strain on his lean face.

'Hello, Fay, may I come in?' he asked quietly, a slight smile curving his firm mouth, as he watched her obvious confusion.

Fay pulled the flimsy wrap tighter around her slender body and took a deep breath. 'I suppose so,' she said breathlessly, unable to control the effect he was having on her.

'Thank you,' he murmured drily, mocking her gently.

She stood back to let him in, keeping a safe distance between them in the tiny hallway. She shut the door and turned to find him staring at her with narrowed eyes.

'Is . . . is that your car outside?' she asked politely, just for something to ease the tension inside her, his dark unwavering stare made her feel uneasy.

Gabriel nodded. 'Your friend next door offered me a drink while I waited for you.'

'Come and sit down,' Fay indicated the lounge. 'I'll just get dressed and then we can talk.'

Gabriel grabbed her wrist, his strong fingers caressing the tiny bones. 'I prefer you like that,' he said softly, his grey eyes clouding, as they slid over her appraisingly. 'Come and talk now.'

Not wanting to provoke a scene, Fay agreed, freeing her wrist and trying to ignore the mocking glint in his eyes as she did so.

They sat by the fire, a few feet away from each other, and she eyed him warily, wondering why he had come to see her. As he lit two cigarettes she watched him carefully from under her lashes, unwilling to reveal the love she felt sure was shining in her eyes every time she looked at him. He looked gaunt, pale, fiercely attractive, his grey eyes burning with a dark fire. He seemed exhausted. The blue shirt he was wearing clung to his powerful body like a second skin, his lean thighs tightly encased in old denim jeans.

'How is Danny?' she asked nervously, her eyes hungry on his face, as she accepted the cigarette he handed her. Gabriel's mouth twisted in the semblance of a smile, a smile that did not reach his burning eyes.

'He's very well, and happier now, I think.'

Fay nodded, feeling acutely uncomfortable. They were acting like strangers, and she felt frightened suddenly.

'Would you like a drink?' she asked, the light, false tone of her own voice making her cringe. 'I'm going to have one.'

She got to her feet carefully, pulling the robe around her tightly.

'Yes, thank you,' he said abruptly, aware of her nervousness.

She moved over to pour the drinks, but her hands were shaking so much that she dropped a glass. Gabriel walked up behind her, silently, his voice near her ear, making her jump. 'Sit down, I'll do that,' he said coolly.

Fay moved away from him quickly, jerkily, still shaking, and obediently sat down, her emerald eyes huge and afraid.

He passed her a glass and returned to his seat indolently, putting distance between them again. Fay could hardly control her desire to go to him, to admit her love for him. He was glancing around the room with interest, taking in the pale walls, rich polished floorboards and Oriental rugs. Then he noticed the pile of his books on the table and turned to her with a slight smile.

'Have you read them?'

'No,' Fay admitted honestly, cursing herself for not putting them away, even though she had not known of his visit.

'Is Sophie well?' she asked, not looking at him, swallowing convulsively, unable to bear the silence.

'Dammit, Fay, I didn't come here to discuss the health of various mutual friends!' Gabriel exploded angrily.

Fay got to her feet and walked over to the window, staring out at the clear evening sky, hurt by his anger.

'What did you come here for?' she whispered brokenly, wrapping her arms around herself in an instinctive gesture of defence. He did not answer, and she could not bear it.

'I don't know what to say to you!' she cried out in anguish, feeling tears warm on her cold face.

Then he was behind her, sliding his arms around her gently. He groaned, feeling her tremble at his touch.

'Oh, Fay, Fay, don't cry, my love,' he said softly against her hair.

She swayed back against his broad shoulders, needing his comfort. She had cried so many times alone.

'Hold me, Gabriel,' she begged with a whisper.

He turned her round in his arms and held her tightly, his lean hands reaching up to stroke tenderly through her burnished hair, soothing her. Fay cried silently against his chest, all her loneliness and longing welling up inside and overwhelming her. She loved him so very much, surely she had the right to be comforted by him. Finally her tears dried and Gabriel tilted her face up with strong sensitive fingers, wiping away her tears and gently stroking her damp face. She sighed softly; it was so good, so sweet to be near him again, dreams had been her only consolation for so long.

Gabriel was still looking down at her, his grey eyes unfathomable beneath heavy lids.

'I shouldn't have come,' he said flatly. 'I upset you—I'm sorry.' He let her go and turned to leave.

Fay thought her heart would stop beating, and desperation flooded over her, fierce misery.

'You still haven't told me why you came,' she said softly, staring at his broad back, unwilling to let him go.

He stopped, still and tense. 'I had to see you again,' he ground out savagely.

Fay's heart soared at his harshly-spoken words. 'Don't go,' she pleaded in a low voice.

He turned to her, his grey eyes tormented. He stared at her for a moment, then with a hoarse groan he was beside her, pulling her against him, his mouth finding hers with fierce expertise. Fay wound her slim arms around his neck, delighting in the thick dark hair beneath her fingers. Her lips parted in surrender beneath the hungry pressure of his, allowing him access to the soft sweetness of her mouth. She quivered as his hands slid over her exploringly, finding her soft bare skin beneath the wrap with trembling urgency. Gabriel was breathing heavily, his heart beneath her stroking fingers, racing away, as he lifted her effortlessly into his arms.

'I want you, Fay—however wrong it is, I want you, I have to have you,' he said thickly, his eyes heavy with desire as they rested on her bruised, parted lips.

Wrong. The word was spinning around in Fay's head

as she lay in his arms. Yes, it was wrong, because he did not love her, because he was going to marry Cecilia, the mother of his child. She stared at him, her emerald eyes dark with pain. 'Let me down,' she ordered coldly, anger rising inside her like a tidal wave.

Gabriel released her immediately and set her gently down on her feet.

'Thinking about the wedding?' he mocked bitterly, his desire well under control now.

Fay turned on him furiously, amazed at the casual way he could talk about his forthcoming marriage, having just released her from his arms.

'Yes, and you're right about all this being wrong. Cecilia deserves your fidelity.'

Gabriel frowned. 'What are you talking about?' he asked irritably.

'Cecilia! I'm talking about Cecilia!' Fay shouted angrily, sure he was playing games with her. 'I'm glad you're marrying her, for Danny's sake!'

Light dawned in Gabriel's grey eyes and his face creased into a smile, then he threw back his dark head and laughed out loud. Fay stared at him impotently.

'You really are incredible!' she choked. 'You come here and try to . . . try to make love to me, and all the time you have responsibilities, that you seem to find very amusing . . . oh!'

He was still laughing and Fay glared at him. Seeing her sweet outraged face he made an effort to control himself.

'Have you quite finished? You really do have an acid tongue!' he said mildly, obviously still amused. 'Danny is not my son, and Cecilia is not his mother, neither is she my lover—she never has been. I have no intention of marrying her. I was talking about your wedding.'

Fay stared at him, wondering at the distaste in his voice.

'My wedding?' she echoed weakly. 'I'm not getting married ... I don't know what you're talking about. What do you mean ... Danny ... and Cecilia ...?' She felt confused, wanting to believe him.

He took her arm and guided her to the couch, sitting down beside her. 'Before I start, tell me one thing, are you going to marry Sam?'

'I told you, I broke off my engagement before I went to Sophie's,' Fay said patiently, not understanding him.

'But you still love him,' Gabriel said bleakly. 'I heard you telling him so, in the kitchen.'

Fay smiled. 'Yes, I love him—he's virtually my brother, and I love him like a brother,' she replied, feeling puzzled. 'Tell me about Danny,' she finished impatiently. Gabriel was smiling at her, as if a great weight had been lifted from his shoulders.

'He's not your lover,' he said quietly, almost to himself.

Fay blushed. 'He's never been my lover, and he's never likely to be.'

'I thought you two had got together again, I thought you were going to be married,' Gabriel said slowly, the words difficult for him to say.

'No, there's no chance of that. When I broke off the engagement we had a terrible row, and when Sam came to Sophie's, I thought it was to try and persuade me to marry him,' she broke off suddenly. 'I'm sorry, you can't possibly be interested in all this,' she said, feeling foolish.

'I am. Tell me,' Gabriel commanded, watching her carefully.

Fay shrugged. 'I knew that I could never marry him, that I loved him like a brother, and I didn't want him to come to Sophie's. But when he came, it was to sort things out, he too had realised what a disaster marriage

would be. I was so relieved that we could be friends
again. That's all. . . . At the moment, he's seeing Angie,
the girl next door, and it might be serious.'

'You don't mind?'

Fay thought for a moment. 'No, I don't. I want him
to be happy, and if Angie's the right girl for him I'm
glad,' she said slowly. Then, shaking his arm, 'Tell me
about Danny,' she repeated, hardly able to contain
herself.

Gabriel lit a cigarette, offering her one, which she
took.

'Did you really think that Danny was my son?' he
asked curiously and almost proudly.

Fay nodded dumbly, feeling ashamed.

'He isn't, although in a way I wish he was. Alex was
his father. His mother, Cecilia's sister—see how com-
plicated it gets?—died in childbirth. She was very ill
before the birth and Danny was particularly difficult
to deliver. Alex went for a doctor, but they were living
up in the mountains at the time, and by the time he
got back it was too late. Alex was out of his mind—
feeling that it was his fault, because he had bought the
house and it was so far from the town, so inaccessible,
and I think that losing Maria made him uncaring for
his own life. He couldn't love Danny as he should have
done because he blamed him, not intentionally of
course, but every time he looked at the baby, he was
reminded. He loved Maria fiercely.' Gabriel's eyes
were distant, reliving the pain of the brother he had
loved so much.

Fay could feel the tears on her face. It was so tragic,
they had all suffered so, especially Danny, born into
the world with no mother, and a father who could not
love him. Small wonder that he was such a sad child.

Gabriel continued, 'Maria's family took Danny from
birth. Alex would see him, of course, but he was not

capable of bringing Danny up, so he sent money and expensive presents instead. After his death, it came out that he had squandered all his money, that he was penniless, and the money stopped—that's why Cecilia came over here. Her family won't keep him any longer unless I pay. I think I would have done, until I saw him and realised what was going on. I had no idea—I guess they haven't been mistreating him, but they sure as hell don't care for him.' His mouth tightened angrily, his eyes as hard as flint. 'You saw how he is— he has nightmares, he's withdrawn, he can't be left alone. I can't let him be brought up like that, he's not a meal ticket for anybody!'

His face became thoughtful as he stared at Fay. 'It's strange—when Alex died, I hardly gave Danny a thought, I was so wrapped up in my own grief, my own guilt ... I imagined that I wouldn't be able to face him, that he would be too much of a reminder. But when Cecilia arrived with him, I felt responsible for him, absurdly protective. . . . He's so easy to love, so like Alex, and I can't let him go. Danny is part of Alex, all that's left of him, and I find that I love him as I would my own son. It's difficult to explain—do you understand?'

Fay nodded. 'But what about Cecilia? She loves you,' she said gently, needing to know.

Gabriel shrugged carelessly. 'Perhaps,' he said arrogantly. 'But I care nothing for her, I never have. She's cold and she's cruel. There was never anything between us—sure, I used to see quite a bit of her, it was inevitable because of Maria and Alex, and she made her feelings clear, but I made mine equally clear, and when she turned up at Sophie's with Danny, it was fairly obvious what she was up to. I'm grateful to her in a way for bringing Danny and me together, for giving me the opportunity to realise just what he means to me. She's gone back to Sicily anyway,' he said dismissively. 'Danny's with Sophie.'

Fay wanted to laugh, happiness bubbled up inside her. She wanted to fling her arms around him and declare her love. She had believed such awful things about him, been always ready to doubt him, to think the worst. She should have known better. She knew now that she had clutched at anything to use against him, to try and kill the love she felt for him. She had wanted him to be cruel and immoral, so that she could justify the fact that he did not return her love. Everything fell into place, now, like a jigsaw. She knew now why Gabriel had refused Cecilia that morning in the lounge when Fay had been listening to their conversation, why he had admitted responsibility for Danny. Also, why Cecilia had been so cold with Danny, and why he had never once called her mother, or shown her any affection. It was all so obvious, why had she never seen it before? How could she have been so blind?

'What will happen to Danny?' she asked sadly.

Gabriel smiled, his deep love for the child warm and gentle in his eyes. 'I hope to adopt him, if——' He broke off suddenly, as if too embarrassed to continue.

Fay stared at him in amazement, wondering what he had been about to say. She sighed miserably. The misunderstandings between them were cleared up, but he did not love her. He wanted her, but desire and love were poles apart. She felt desperate. Soon he would walk out of the flat, and out of her life, for ever probably, and she could not bear it. She could not let him go. He was watching her tensely with narrowed eyes. She turned to him, licking her lips nervously, intending to do something that she had never expected to find herself doing.

'Gabriel . . .' she began falteringly, 'you said that you wanted me . . . you said . . . you made me admit how it is between us, I do admit it now ... I want you.'

He did not move, merely sat perfectly still, not speaking, staring at her with dark intent eyes. Hectic colour washed up her face. Was he going to reject her? She wished she had not spoken. Love had made her so weak, had she really thought that if they had an affair, he would come to love her? She bowed her head. 'I won't beg,' she said steadily. 'If you don't want me. . . .'

Gabriel groaned. 'Want you?' he muttered through clenched teeth. 'I've lain awake so many nights, aching for you. I've been crazy with wanting you,' he admitted roughly. 'I wanted to kill you when you told me that you were engaged, when I found you in Sam's arms admitting your love for him.'

Fay lifted her head, catching the violence in his eyes as he reached for her. He was jealous! Surely that meant he cared for her? Gabriel buried his face in her thick, soft hair. He was shaking.

'I don't want just an affair. I want more than your body, Fay, I want your heart, your love, everything. Tell me you love me, Fay,' he groaned. 'Oh God, tell me you love me, as much as I love you.'

She pushed at his broad chest, staring into his face, her breath coming in short uneven gasps, hardly able to believe her ears. 'I love you, Gabriel, I love you so badly it hurts,' she said softly, her green eyes burning with her love.

He sighed hoarsely with contentment, reaching to cup her face in his gentle hands.

'And I love you,' he said thickly. 'I think I've always loved you.' He lowered his dark head slowly, the silver glitter of his eyes making her head spin as their mouths touched. Their kiss was fierce, Gabriel's mouth hardening with passion as her lips parted. Hunger and love strained them closer, his hands urgent, trembling as he loosened her wrap, finding her soft nakedness beneath with a violent groan of pleasure. His mouth became almost desperate, as his lean, strong fingers stroked over her body, making her shudder with intense pleasure.

Needing to touch him in return, Fay reached for him, fumbling with the buttons of his shirt, until the warm, hair-roughened skin of his chest was beneath her hands. She sighed with pleasure, caressing the hard muscles and smooth skin of his body with love.

She heard him groan, breathing hard as she touched him, her hands moving over him with confidence, her palms flat as she shaped the tense muscles of his shoulders. His mouth left hers to trail hungrily over her body, leaving a path of fire on her skin, his hands cupped her breasts, stroking and arousing with trembling expertise. He shuddered, his heart pounding.

'I've waited so long for you,' he murmured unsteadily against her mouth. 'God, Fay, you're so beautiful!' He lifted his head reluctantly, a possessive smile curving his mouth, his eyes molten with love and desire. 'You're mine,' he asserted softly, 'and I'll never let you go. You'll marry me—tomorrow if possible. God knows, I can't wait much longer for you.'

Fay laughed, touched deeply by his words. 'You're old-fashioned,' she accused teasingly.

He arched over her, his eyes warning.

'You want to bet?' he threatened gently.

'Tomorrow will do fine,' she giggled breathlessly. Then, 'Hold me, Gabriel,' she pleaded.

He pushed the fabric from between them and held her close, their bodies came together sweetly, as if they had been made for each other. Fay sighed achingly as she lay in his arms.

'I'd resigned myself to living without you,' she whispered against his strong brown throat. 'I seem to have loved you for ever.'

Gabriel stared down at her, his grey eyes disturbing. 'I missed you like hell when you left,' he admitted huskily. 'I had to see you again, even though I thought you hated me, after that row over Sophie's house. I came here to stop you marrying Sam, to tell you that I loved you, needed you, I couldn't let you go.'

'Sophie told me about the house,' Fay explained. 'I was fighting my feelings for you all the time. I'm so sorry I accused you of all those terrible things.'

Gabriel laughed low in his throat, making her shiver.

'I'll make you pay,' he murmured thickly, moulding her closer to his warm hard body.

She kissed his shoulder. 'I hated you for being so honest,' she remembered. 'Right from the beginning you forced me to acknowledge my love for you, and I was afraid because my feelings were so intense. I lied to you because I was afraid of giving myself away.'

'I loved you even then,' Gabriel told her. 'The first time we met, I watched you on the station, fragile and alone, so very lovely. I knew that I would have you—I had to have you.' His voice had become rough and possessive.

Fay stroked his back gently, running her nails lightly over his smooth skin, delighting in his shuddering response.

'You have me,' she whispered in surrender.

'Not completely,' he replied huskily, his lips erotic against her ear. 'But soon. . . .'

'We argued all the time—always anger and passion. We could never be friends,' Fay sighed.

'I wanted you so much, my love, it was driving me mad,' Gabriel admitted ruefully. 'I was angry because I thought you were engaged. Every time I saw you I was reminded that you belonged to him, it was like a knife turning slowly in my stomach. I was cruel to you, hurting you instinctively, as you were hurting me—forgive me. I didn't want to be cruel, I swear to you.'

Fay snuggled closer. 'I know. I never meant to lie, it was my only defence whenever you kissed me.'

'I kissed you so often, not only because I couldn't resist you but because I wanted to make you see what was between us. I didn't want to break your engagement, I wanted you to do it,' he said wickedly.

Fay laughed. 'You certainly made me jealous,' she accused. 'Lucy Baxter all over you, Cecilia obviously in love with you. She warned me away from you, did you know?'

'I didn't,' Gabriel said curtly, his mouth tightening. 'I've told you about Cecilia, and Lucy——' he snorted, 'she's only a child. Perhaps I was trying to make you jealous, but I need a woman. You.' He kissed her fiercely, leaving her in no doubt of his feelings.

'What about all the women I've read about in the newspapers?' Fay asked painfully.

Gabriel touched her face gently. 'Most of that is publicity—don't believe newspapers. There have been women, I can't deny that, but what I felt for them can never compare with what I feel for you, Fay. I've never loved as I love you, and there'll never be anybody else,' he promised, offering her his fidelity for life, reassuring her.

'Besides,' he growled tenderly, 'you put me through hell with jealousy when Sam turned up and you were forever in his arms. I wanted to strangle him with my bare hands.'

'He knew I loved you. He comforted me when it hurt, when I couldn't stand the thought of Cecilia being the mother of your child. Danny is so like you, Gabriel. I think that's one of the reasons I love him so much. Please adopt him and let him live with us,' she begged, with shining eyes.

'You wouldn't mind?' Gabriel watched her carefully, his eyes serious.

Fay shook her head vigorously.

'No, I want him to be with us, and perhaps we. . . .' Her voice trailed off, and she blushed furiously. Gabriel held her tightly, reading her mind, enchanted by her shyness.

'I want you to bear my child, our child,' he said in a low voice, and Fay felt shaken inside by his intensity. He kissed her hard, then leaned back to look at her, his silver eyes laying bare his soul for her to take and keep.

'I'm taking you out to dinner now,' he asserted huskily. 'I can't take much more of this—it's driving me crazy, having you so near.'

Fay smiled the smile of a temptress, encircling his strong neck with her slim white arms.

'I'll cook something for us later. I want to stay here with you,' she said provocatively.

'Do you know what will happen?' he asked huskily, eyeing her with undisguised and hungry desire.

'Yes,' Fay replied, leaning forward to kiss his mouth. 'Beautiful, perfect passion.'

Gabriel groaned, unable to resist her, and for a long time silence reigned in the warm room.

It had been a long fight, but they had come together at last.

Harlequin Plus
THE LUXURY OF SILK

The soft touch of silk next to the skin is one luxury that many Harlequin heroines—in fact, most women—find irresistible. And fabrics woven from silk have been around for centuries, with some of history's most magnificent costumes fashioned from it—first in the Orient and later in Europe. The ancients are said to have prized it highly, often exchanging silk, weight for weight, for pure gold.

The silk industry reached Europe in the twelfth century, first in Sicily and later in Italy, France and Spain. Silk was not manufactured in England, however, until 1605, when some skilled French refugees established themselves there.

Silk owes its beginnings to the lowly silkworm, of course, a creature indigenous to China. The silkworm is, in fact, a small caterpillar that hatches from the egg of a species of moth. Like any other caterpillar, it is virtually an eating machine, growing rapidly in size as it munches its way through leaf after leaf. When fat and fully grown, the silkworm secretes liquid silk, which solidifies around the worm to form a cocoon.

Man learned long ago to separate the soft silk from the silkworm—by immersing the cocoon in hot water—then to spin it into thread and weave the thread into fabric. Now a highly sophisticated industry with millions of commercial silkworms feasting on mounds of mulberry leaves, the process of silk-making is fascinating—and extremely profitable. Today, the world's chief silk-manufacturing nations are China, Japan, Korea, Italy and the Soviet Union, but fortunate wearers are women the world over.

Harlequin ❖ Salutes...

JANET DAILEY

...with 6 more of her bestselling Presents novels!

Once again Harlequin is proud to salute Janet Dailey, one of the world's most popular romance authors. Now's your chance to discover 6 of Janet Dailey's best—6 great love stories that will intrigue you, captivate you and thrill you as only Harlequin romances can!

Available in May wherever paperback books are sold, or through **Harlequin Reader Service:**

In the U.S.
1440 South Priest Drive
Tempe, AZ 85281

In Canada
649 Ontario Street
Stratford, Ontario N5A 6W2

❧❧ FREE ❧❧
*Harlequin Reader Service Catalog**

A complete listing of all titles currently available in Harlequin Romance, Harlequin Presents, Classic Library and Superromance.

Special offers and exciting new books, too!

*Catalog varies each month.

Complete and mail this coupon today!

Your FREE gift includes

Sweet Revenge by **Anne Mather**
Devil in a Silver Room by **Violet Winspear**
Gates of Steel by **Anne Hampson**
No Quarter Asked by **Janet Dailey**